Amber in December

A Christmas Novella

To Roger,
Thank you for all your help with this story!
Best wishes
Gavin

17/12/24

GAVIN EYERS

© Gavin Eyers 2024

The right of Gavin Eyers to be identified as the author of this work has been asserted by him in accordance with the Copyright, Designs and Patents Act, 1988.

All rights reserved. No part of this work may be reproduced without written permission from the author.

Cover design by Creative Covers.

Cover images Nata_Alhontess/Shutterstock.com and Subbotina Anna/Shutterstock.com

ISBN: 9798327397880

Amber in December and all characters, events and locations are fictional.

Printed in Great Britain
by Amazon

1st December

When I tell people I work in an office in town, they might imagine a high-rise made of glass, with immaculately dressed colleagues sipping expensive coffee and a receptionist who's always pleased to see everyone. Where I actually work is tucked behind one of those glassy high-rises in a squat seventies block. Three storeys of grubby concrete, metal-framed windows, draughts, and a kitchen with a barely functional kettle and splattered microwave. Our receptionist hates us.

It has taken me half an hour to find the Christmas boxes in our junk-filled storeroom. As I place them on my desk, a few people come forward to investigate, and hopefully help put the decorations up. A couple volunteer to look for the tree, which I had no luck in finding. It's a bit early for all this, but today there's been the first hint of festivity here: advent calendars have appeared on some of the desks, including mine of course. First doors have been opened.

'How will you be spending Christmas, Daniel?' Marie, my manager, is looking at me. In her hands is a tangle of tree lights.

'I dunno. Maybe at my mate Spencer's place.' I unwrap another newspaper bundle and find another bauble.

'Not with your mum?'

'No, she and the boyfriend are going away for Christmas this year. Australia.'

'Lucky them.'

'Tell me about it. How about you?'

'At home with the family. The girls are more enthusiastic than ever this year – they're old enough to appreciate it all properly now.'

Though I've met them in passing a few times, I only really know Marie's twins from her stories and from the framed photo beside her monitor. 'Must be very exciting for them.'

'They're talking about it all day, every day.'

Her saying that makes me remember the last Christmas that Mum, Dad, Pete and I all spent together. It was perfect in my memory. 'When we were kids, my little brother and I used to look forward to it all so much.'

Marie looks at me with compassion. 'How is Peter?'

She knows, though happy for him, that I was gutted when he moved from here in England to Canada, with his lovely Canadian wife.

'He's doing well, thanks.'

'And your nephew?'

'He's great!' Speaking of Owen always brings a smile to my face. He's a five-year-old parcel of energy and light. 'I'm hoping to visit them again next year.' Canada, and the three of them, feel a long way from this dull office.

'I found it!'

I turn and see Norman from Customer Services carrying the artificial tree across the office towards us, as though it's a prize he's just won.

'Good man,' I say.

Together we press each of the branches down, try to get a natural effect. Marie has untangled the lights. Having tested they're still working, she presents them to us. I

unfurl them from her hands, while Norman strings them around the tree carefully and evenly. We hang the baubles and little stars that we dress this tree with every year. Then, the fairy, who it seems was packed at the bottom of a box last year. Marie unbends her, then places her on top of the tree.

The rest of the decorations are hung: accordion paper bells, a garland that stretches over the desk dividers, an angel mobile, a pine cone and red ribbon wreath for the kitchen door. Tinsel everywhere that it can be attached by a drawing pin. We display the wooden nativity set on top of a filing cabinet. Marie finds the elf hat: the hat has worked here for more Christmases than me. It smells musty, and Marie must notice it too as she turns her nose up, then hangs it on one of the coat hooks before rubbing her hands together to vanish the invisible dirt. I expect that at some point in December someone will be tempted to put that hat on, and will, until they smell it.

'There,' Marie says, smiling as she looks across the office. 'Brightened the place up a bit, hasn't it?'

I can't deny that it has. 'It's the start of Christmas!' I say, a little too loudly, trying to initiate some excitement.

Nathaniel from Marketing returns a woo-hoo. Tim the office junior rolls his eyes and sighs. The rest are tapping away on their keyboards. Marie and I put the empty boxes and packaging into the storeroom.

The afternoon passes a bit slowly, but it's OK as I've got plenty of work to get through. At five I quickly get changed into my cycle gear in the loo.

'Bye, see you tomorrow,' I call, as I pass through Reception. The receptionist, busy doing something, blanks

me, which is OK because she always blanks me, and everyone, but all the same I'd feel rude walking past her without saying anything.

After I've unchained my bike, I'm pedalling home through town, dodging the rush hour pedestrians who cross without looking. Christmas lights are everywhere. Shops have festive displays in their windows. It's not long before I'm cycling through the rows of terraced houses of the estate, towards one of the two towering blocks of flats: home. I'm nearly there, when I have to brake suddenly. A fox has come out of the darkness and onto the path. At the sound of my screeching brakes it turns to me, though it hasn't run away. We look one another in the eye for a moment before it calmly trots off, glancing back at me once more.

As I continue towards the flats, again I think back to that Christmas all those years ago, to Pete and me. Everything was different then.

Boys

We were in the living room of our little two-bedroom house on the estate. Mum and Dad were having their traditional Christmas Eve brandy. Mum only sipped hers, unlike Dad, who topped his up every now and then.

Pete and I had changed into our pyjamas earlier than usual.

'Can we have our chocolate now, please?' I asked. This was another tradition: me and Pete picking one of the foil-wrapped chocolates from the tree.

'Of course you can, love,' Mum said.

We jumped off the sofa. I chose one, lifted the gold string and carefully passed it over the needles of the branch. Pete wasn't quite so delicate and the tree wobbled as he took his.

We were silent as we ate. The chocolatey paste lining my mouth, I looked over to the many cards we'd received which crowded on every shelf, on the bookcase, on top of the TV. The house was filled with glittery decorations. In the hallway, a spray of mistletoe was stuck to the ceiling. Beside the phone was a sheet of paper with the names of people Mum had to remember to call in the morning to wish them a Merry Christmas. After the calls, she'd knock on the door of our neighbour, Mr Silver, and give him the bottle of sherry that sat on the sideboard in a twist of blue tissue paper.

Pete cupped his hand to my ear. 'Dan the Man, do you think we should go to bed now?'

I glanced at the clock, and nodded. 'We're off to bed,' I announced.

'The one night of the year you volunteer to go,' Mum said.

'They have to,' Dad added, 'or *he* won't come.'

Pete ran upstairs.

I was pleased he'd gone, as I needed to check a few things out. I'd been hearing some worrying rumours at school about Father Christmas. I went over to Dad's armchair as casually as possible, slipping my hands into my pyjama pockets. 'So, how does he get in, Dad, when we've got a gas fire?'

'I've told you before, Dan. As we haven't got a proper chimney he knocks on the front door very quietly, and I let him in.'

'So you actually meet him, and actually speak to him, then?'

'Yep.'

'And how is there enough time for him to get to every house in one night?'

Dad looked to Mum, then to me again. 'It's the magic of Christmas,' he said, as if that answered everything.

'And how does he land his sleigh when there's no snow?' I thought this would be the real decider, that'd definitely catch Dad out if there was anything iffy going on.

'Well,' he said, glancing at the carpet for a moment, then back to me. 'The grass is very dewy this time of year, very slippery. He lands the sleigh by sliding it, out there on the green.' He pointed to the closed curtain. 'And while they wait for him, the reindeer feed on the grass. I looked out the window and saw them doing just that last year.

Great big antlers they had.' He raised his hands above his head, antler-like.

I immediately remembered what I'd seen that morning. 'There's dog shit on the green, Dad, I saw it earlier, and if the reindeer are going to land out there and maybe even feed out there, then I'm very worried that—'

I grabbed my left bum cheek. 'Ouch!' I said, just to make a point, as it'd only been a warning swing and hadn't really hurt.

Mum was replacing her slipper, and frowning. 'Don't swear, Daniel!'

'Sorry, Mum,' I said, though really there were more important things to worry about. 'It's true, Dad. There's a massive turd out there.'

Dad was smirking. 'Dan, these guys can fly through the sky at night! Can find their way all around the world while pulling a sleigh full of presents. Do you think they can't sniff out and avoid a dog poo when they need to?'

I had nothing to come back with, as what Dad was saying totally made sense.

'I'm sure everything will be fine, Dan. Trust me?'

I thought for a moment. Then I nodded. If there was one person in the world I trusted, it was Dad. He held up his hand and I high-fived it. 'Night, Dad.'

I glanced at Mum as I headed for the door.

'Where's my kiss?' she said.

I sighed, went back across the living room.

She hugged me tightly and gave me a big, noisy kiss, which made me giggle. 'Goodnight, love.'

'Night, Mum.'

When I reached our bedroom Pete was at the turntable,

placing the needle onto a record.

'You'll have to play it really low, so they don't hear downstairs,' I said. 'And only once, then we'll have to sleep.'

It was Cliff Richard's 'Mistletoe and Wine'. Mum had bought Pete the seven-inch a week before and he'd been playing it non-stop ever since.

'I'm just giving Father Christmas a sign, that's all.'

'A sign for what?'

'That we're here.'

I wondered whether it was really possible that my little brother's record would be heard, that Father Christmas would be reminded that there were two small boys in the small bedroom of our small terraced house, who had at least tried to be good all year. I sat cross-legged on the floor beside Pete, and we listened to Cliff as we watched the record spin, until it finished and the arm returned to rest.

'I think he'll know anyway, Pete,' I said, as I sat on my bed and pulled the blankets back.

'How will he?'

'It's the *magic of Christmas*. OK? It just happens.'

'But how do you know?'

'How old are you, Pete?'

'Five years and four months and three days.'

'And how old am I?'

'Eight.'

'So I'm older. That's how I know.'

'All right then,' Pete said. He turned off our lamp, then climbed up the ladder to his bunk. As he dropped onto his mattress above me, the whole frame shook, the way it did

every night when he got in. 'Night,' he said.

'Night, Pete.'

I was beginning to feel tired, and thought: what if they didn't hear the front door when he knocked? Would he simply skip us and move onto Mr Silver next door? I was nervous at the prospect that Pete might not get the BMX he was hoping for, nor me the cassette tape player I wanted. But I trusted Dad would manage it all.

Pete fell asleep quickly as always, his snoring light and slow.

I wondered if anything would be going on outside, though it might be too early. I lifted my head; Pete didn't like the curtains closed as he was afraid of the dark, but from where I lay I could see only the night sky through the window, and the moonlight cast across our bedroom wall.

I felt sleepy, my mind full of pictures: his heavy black boots walking along the path, his big white beard, the sack of presents slung over his shoulder. His reindeer, a bit big and scary. I wondered what their fur might feel like.

Just as sleep was taking me away, I thought that, distantly, perhaps from the green, I heard the tinkle of sleigh bells.

3rd December

I'm cycling home in sunshine, having met Spencer for a Saturday morning gym session. I didn't sleep well, but I feel fresh after my workout. I'm ready for the day ahead even though I've nothing big planned, other than opening the community centre on the estate tonight, where the other volunteers and I are hosting a darts competition. My weekends are quieter than my weekdays.

I swing round the side of the flats and push my bike into the tower lobby. I whistle as I wait for the lift. Inside, I press *15*. The doors close. I'm swept upwards.

In my flat, I lean my bike then grab the post from the mat. A couple of early Christmas cards. Another envelope which, I know without opening, is my mobile phone bill. The final envelope isn't for me. It's for someone called Amber. Then I see the address. 'Oh, it's *her…*' I whisper. She lives a few floors below me – I'm in flat 157 and she's in 117 – the postie must have mixed our letters up. I've never met her properly, even though I know which flat she lives in; it's a small world this big tower block, plus she's caught my attention more than most. I feel a bit guilty as I tilt the envelope to the light, try to guess what it might contain, to see whether it gives any clue about her life. Nothing.

I go to the end of the landing and head downstairs. Somewhere, perhaps way below or far above, conversation and laughter echo. The stairs in this block are a realm of their own. Sometimes there are teenagers here, smoking or

writing on the walls. Other times, acts of kindness, like the day I saw some lads carrying shopping up for an old resident when the lift was broken. Once, someone was found here beaten up. More than once I've passed by a couple enjoying the moment.

I arrive on the eleventh floor. It's strange how each landing is so different. Here, there are doormats, a cat's food and water bowls and some lovely big houseplants in pots. These plants have been here for years. That simply wouldn't happen on the fifteenth. A few months back, I left my muddy trainers outside my door. Half an hour later, they were gone. For weeks I gave the teenagers the eye as I passed them, to see if I could spot who'd taken them. I was stunned one day to see them on the elderly lady who lives on the sixteenth, who was walking a bit quicker than usual and smirked as she went past me.

As I approach 117, I feel nervous. Although I'm only here to deliver a letter, it's as though there's some other motive for me rushing down the stairs. Just as I'm reaching for the letterbox, there's a sound, and the door opens. 'Oh,' I say, stupidly.

'Hi,' Amber says, looking a bit surprised to see me. She's wearing a coat and a hat and is apparently on her way out.

'I was just going to put something through your letterbox,' I say, holding the envelope out as proof. 'I live upstairs. It came through my door by mistake.'

'Thanks,' she says, taking the letter. There's nothing on her wedding finger. 'That's kind of you to bring it down.'

'No problem,' I say, backing away. 'Have a wonderful day.' I head for the stairs.

'Bye!' she calls.

I jump the steps two at a time, wishing I hadn't told her to have a wonderful day when it's just an odd thing to say. I'm relieved when I'm back in my flat. 'That was embarrassing,' I mutter to myself, pulling my jacket off as I go to the kitchen.

The gym has left me starving. I go to the fridge and take some food that I made last night, then go to the living room. I eat as I look through the balcony doors. If there's one thing that can be said for this flat, it's the view. Either side of the opposite tower I can see for miles, especially on a crisp morning like this. I see hundreds of buildings, some nearby, some distant and tiny.

I open a door, step outside and look towards the ground, to the green. I see a fox, sniffing the grass and wandering around, looking a little out of place in daylight. I wonder if it's the same one I saw the other night. Then on one of the pathways I notice Amber on her way to wherever she's off to, maybe a lunch date with some lucky guy. She's soon out of sight amongst the houses. One of those little terraced houses is where Mum, Pete and I used to live – and Dad until he left us that January for the new girlfriend he'd met in the pub. For months we heard Mum crying through our bedroom wall. Before that though, and after when there was just the three of us, the memories of my childhood were made down there in that house.

Back inside, I need to occupy myself. I head down the hallway and into the spare box bedroom. I say bedroom; there's no bed here, just a few boxes of junk and my workbench, where there's a piece of lime wood I bought the other day. I turn the wood over and over in my hands,

getting a feel for it, picturing things. I don't yet know what it'll become.

The Gift

I was still young, about twelve I think, when a few days before Christmas I noticed an oddly shaped present beneath the tree. The tag was addressed to me, from Mr Silver next door. Every year he had a present for each of us, maybe because he and Mum were more like friends than neighbours. She'd pick things up for him when she was shopping: a loaf, a block of cheese or a bag of apples. He was quite old, but after Dad left he was always happy to lend a hand if something in the house needed repairing or replacing. I think he felt sorry for us.

Pete also had a gift from Mr Silver, and after weighing and shaking it we'd decided that it was a sweetie selection pack. But we couldn't even guess at what mine might be. The parcel had a rounded part and a sticky-out part. It was quite heavy and wrapped in paper covered with pictures of holly leaves. We placed our presents back under the tree, alongside those from Mum. We knew that we got only one each from her, because money had been tight since Dad. We didn't go on holiday or even for days out any more. No chocolate spread.

Mr Silver's gift intrigued me so much that on Christmas morning, after Pete and I woke up and went storming downstairs, that odd package was the first thing I grabbed. I ripped the holly wrapping, and after a few seconds, the paper dropping to the carpet, I was holding a wooden carving of a bird. A duck, actually. I knew the species; mallards lived on 'the ditch', which was what the little

stream that ran alongside the estate was known as, even though it didn't have a name. As I looked closely, I found that each feather was precisely carved. It was smooth underneath – I guessed so that it could sit on a cupboard or shelf and appear that it was swimming. Its head was turned slightly to one side as if it was observing something; its eyes looked at me. I don't know what I expected the present to be, but it wasn't *that*. I felt a bit jealous as I turned and saw Pete unwrapping his selection pack.

Mum came into the living room, wearing her dressing gown. 'Wow, let's have a look,' she said. She took the duck from me. 'It's beautiful. Mr Silver told me he was making this for you.'

I looked to the duck, then back at Mum. I sensed that I should be amazed by the present, be extremely grateful for it, but I couldn't say anything. I appreciated Mr Silver's thought, because it was clear an awful lot of time and care had gone into this wooden mallard. But I couldn't understand why he, or anyone, would put so much effort into something when they could have just gone and bought something else better from the shop. I took the duck, placed it on the floor and reached for my other present, from Mum. I knew this one was going to be the *Now That's What I Call Music! 23* cassette I really wanted, as I'd been going on about it for weeks and had even pointed it out to her in Our Price, to make sure she got the right one.

Later that morning, Mum started making dinner. Pete and I offered to help, we always did, but we knew really that the best thing we could do was to stay out of her way. The sound of her stress in the kitchen was such a part of Christmas Day that we'd have been worried if we couldn't

hear it. The smell of roasting food was wafting through the house before long, even though Mum screamed the F-word at the turkey every now and then for not cooking properly.

Pete and I got to work on our *thank you* cards for Mum and Mr Silver. We sat on the living room floor with felt-tip pens and sheets of paper all around us, my new cassette playing, that duck watching us, and all the while we looked forward to dinner. We were excited for the crackers we'd pull, and the pudding. I loved the whole ceremony of it, the way we only had this dinner once a year, how the stuffing balls tasted with cranberry sauce on them, the Yorkshires splashed with gravy.

After washing up, Pete and I, wrapped in our coats and hats and scarves and gloves, knocked on Mr Silver's door. It was dark by then, Mum's dinner having taken hours longer than planned, like it always did. We waited in the pool of light from the lamp at his porch. It was a little while before he opened the door, but when he did he looked pleased to see us.

'Merry Christmas, Mr Silver!' Pete yelled. There was still something babyish in the way Pete shouted at times, as if his volume didn't work properly.

I had got suddenly taller that year, and my voice deeper, and as I added, 'Merry Christmas, Mr Silver,' I did so in a calm, more grown-up way than Pete. I liked to make the point sometimes that I was the older brother.

'Merry Christmas, boys,' he said.

We both held our envelopes towards him. He knew what was inside them, of course – he got a thank-you-for-

our-present card from us every year.

'Very kind,' he said. 'And thank your mum again for my bottle of sherry, will you? I've already opened it!'

'Will do,' I said.

'Thank you for my selection pack,' Pete said.

I was a bit embarrassed then, felt I should say something about my wooden duck carving. I just didn't know what to say about it, so I said, 'Goodnight, Mr Silver,' and Pete and I headed home.

By Boxing Day, the mallard was in the big storage chest in our bedroom. It got buried in toys and junk, and for a long time I only ever saw that wooden duck by chance when I was searching for something else.

5th December

In the town centre, there's a giant Christmas tree that people are stopping to appreciate or have their photo taken beside. The scent of roasting chestnuts and something sugary wafts from the market at the end of town. It's crowded, but everyone seems cheerful. A different place here at this time of year, with the lights and music.

The shops are open late tonight, as they are twice a week through December for Christmas shopping. I can take my time, as I only have a few presents to buy. Weeks ago, I ordered a hamper to be delivered for Spencer and his wife Joanne. For Mum and Ricardo, I booked an excursion, arranged in secret with Ricardo, and he'll surprise Mum with it during their holiday in Australia. That leaves the four other people in my life to buy gifts for tonight: Pete, my sister-in-law Camille, little Owen, and Spencer and Joanne's daughter, my god-daughter, Daisy-May.

I go into a clothes shop. Pete is easy to buy for, as we have the same tastes. We wear the same size, too, as my little brother not only grew as tall as me but overtook me by one inch. Our similar build meant that by the time we were teenagers we'd share and swap our clothes, which was something we did right up until he moved to Canada.

I choose a jumper, burgundy with a bold white stripe across the chest and sleeves. The wool is thick and heavy, so it'll be useful for him – I experienced how cold the winters are there when I visited them last year. After

finding a size medium, I slip my jacket off and try the jumper on. It fits perfectly.

As I queue for the till, my mind goes back to that holiday in Canada. I had magical days out with Owen. Pete, Camille and I enjoyed late evenings in front of their fireplace with food and hot drinks, conversation and laughter. I leave the shop with my first present bagged and a warm feeling in my chest.

Last week on the phone, I asked Pete what I could buy for Camille. He'd suggested earrings, said she'd been saying she doesn't have enough, though I think really he might just be trying to save me some money on the post with something small and light.

As I step into the jewellers, I'm greeted by a shop assistant offering me a chocolate. 'Thank you,' I say, as I take an orange creme, but only because I can't see a purple one and I don't think it'd be right for me to start digging through the tin. 'Wonderful Christmastime' is coming from the speakers as I go to the counter. The young guy behind it is wearing a Father Christmas hat.

'How can I help you?' he asks.

'I'd like to buy a pair of earrings for my sister-in-law.'

'What type does she wear?'

I think about this. 'Silver, never gold. And nothing too big.'

'I'll be right back,' he says.

He returns with a tray, dark blue and cushioned, where earrings are displayed in neat rows. I consider them carefully, the hoops and animals, the flowers and studs. I try to picture how each would look on Camille, wonder which she'd most like to receive.

'Those ones, please,' I say, pointing to the little trails of stars.

'Lovely.' He gently picks them up and places them into a box.

'Merry Christmas,' he says as I leave the shop with another present bagged.

'Merry Christmas,' I return, though really I think it's a bit early in the month for all that.

The toy shop is next, where I'll get the most important gifts. I've been here a few times over recent weeks, checking out the options and buying a few things. I wouldn't mind another browse now, but it's probably for the best that I already know what I can buy as the shop is packed tonight. For Owen, I get a jigsaw puzzle, a pop-up book and a pack of snap cards. He likes unwrapping presents more than anything – it's definitely a case of quantity over quality for Owen. I get a colouring book for him too. These things are to go along with those I've already bought and have at home: a felt-tip set, a calendar with pictures of birds, a jacket. I know the jacket is going to be Owen's favourite. He's strangely fashion-conscious for a five-year-old.

In the craft department I pick up a bracelet-making set for Daisy-May, which I think, I hope, she'll enjoy. She's always creating things. Spencer often turns up at the gym with something homemade, a painting or drawing, that she's sent for me.

I leave the toy shop and find that it's got dark. It's chilly now, too. My breath is white steam as I walk along High Street in the direction of the Christmas market. I take my time as I look at the lights that hang above the road, that sit

on building fronts, that dangle from lampposts. This year's display of snowflakes isn't bad at all, though the jumping reindeer of three Christmases ago are yet to be beaten.

I notice that most people here are with others. I've got used to doing things on my own, but once in a while it bothers me, even though I'm not alone in life. And every Christmas, Spencer and Joanne invite me to their place for the day. Though I love spending time with them and Daisy-May, I usually have Christmas at Mum's house. With Mum and Ricardo being away, I'll gratefully accept Spencer and Joanne's invite this year.

The sheds at the Christmas market are brightly lit, colourful, are selling decorations and gifts, fragrant mulled wine and all kinds of food. I buy a pancake rolled with chocolate, then carry it over to one of the nearby tables and set my shopping down beside me.

My healthy eating all goes wrong around Christmastime. There's always a moment where the turning point happens... and it just has. I'd forgotten how good these things taste. I'm already putting the last piece in and licking my fingers. I've devoured it.

I'm dabbing my lips with a napkin when I notice Amber, some distance away, walking by the shops on the opposite side of the road. She stops outside the little supermarket, slips her headphones off, then leans down to speak to a homeless lady who sits in a sleeping bag and leans against the wall. The lady looks up at Amber and says something. Amber nods, then she's gone into the shop.

I have finished my food and I've no reason to be standing here any more, but I don't want to leave this spot, where I'm sure Amber won't notice me, might not

recognise me or think enough of it to say hello if she did. After all, I'm just that guy who brought a misdelivered letter to her.

It's a good five minutes before she leaves the shop, a sandwich and a big bag of crisps in one hand, in the other a hot drink cup. She gives them to the lady. They speak a short while before they wave goodbye. Amber puts her headphones back on, then is lost among the crowds. My heart is light from the kindness I've just witnessed.

Mr Silver

I was fourteen when I came across the wooden mallard, buried in the chest in our bedroom. It had got a bit scratched in the time since Mr Silver had given it to me. There was a small dent on its head. One of the wings had been partly coloured with green pen, for which the only suspect was Pete. I turned the carving in my hands, looked closely at the fine detail of its feathers. The duck seemed as though it was actually looking at me. Its closed bill was so realistic that it might open and quack at any moment. Folded wings appeared as if they could unfurl and fly.

I carried it to the living room. After making space amongst Mum's china and brass, I placed the mallard on top of the cabinet. I stood back to check its position was good enough just as Mum, still wearing her waitress apron, arrived home from work.

She was surprised when she saw the duck. 'Where did you find that?'

'At the bottom of the toy chest. I thought we might as well have it out on show here.'

'You couldn't stand it when you got it!'

'Maybe I didn't appreciate it at the time.' I didn't want to let Mum know she was altogether right.

'You've grown up a bit since then,' she said.

I looked back to the mallard. 'I'd love to be able to make something like this.'

'Ask Mr Silver to teach you.'

'I haven't seen him for ages,' I said, though that wasn't

entirely true. No one else knew that, a few weeks before, I'd been in his house.

'I'm sure he won't mind.'

After school the following day, I was sitting on Mr Silver's sofa. The wooden duck was in a carrier bag beside me. Mr Silver was in his kitchen, making us tea after he'd refused my help to do so. I wished he'd accepted my help – he was becoming elderly. He had a sister and nieces, and even a new-born great-nephew, Luke, a framed photo of whom sat on the sideboard, but they all lived a long way away, so Mr Silver only really had us next door.

I thought back to my recent visit to his house. Mum, Pete and I had heard that Dad and his girlfriend were having a baby. In the years since Dad left, I always thought, hoped, that he might return, but I knew for sure then that he was never coming home. I tried not to be upset, to be strong for Mum and Pete, but I couldn't sleep properly at nights, felt angry during the day, and all I wanted to do was cry my eyes out. I knocked on Mr Silver's door one afternoon, while Mum was at work for a few hours and Pete was playing football on the green. I told Mr Silver everything that was on my mind, about Dad and about life and about myself. He'd let me cry, and told me that everything was going to be OK.

He limped back into the living room, lowered the tea tray onto the table then began to pour from the teapot. As he spooned sugar and splashed milk, stirred, I noticed his big hands with their aged skin, scratches and barely there scars. I thought of all the carvings those hands had made over the years, of the many hours they'd spent making

them.

He settled into his armchair.

I took the mallard from the bag.

'You've still got that?'

'I have.' Feeling awkward, I tried to remember the words I'd prepared and practised a few times before I'd gone to his house. 'Mum said you might not mind showing me how to carve something myself.'

The only sound, a ticking clock.

A smile appeared at the corner of his lips.

That was the start of the summer I spent with Mr Silver. After tea, he took me down to the shed at the end of his garden, or his workshop as he called it. It had a big window, essential for natural light, he said. On the wall, so many tools hung on hooks. On top of the worn, well-used workbench were a few pencils and a metal ruler. A smell of wood shavings was in the air. The workshop felt magical, and instead of being in the middle of the estate, it was as though I'd just walked through a door into another world.

In the corner was a large box that held pieces of wood of all shapes and sizes. Mr Silver dug around in it for a while, before handing me a chunk.

'That,' he said, 'is not a piece of wood.' His words were clear, his expression serious. 'It is an opportunity to bring something into existence.'

I looked down at the piece of wood in my hands. Confused, I looked back up at Mr Silver.

'Don't worry,' he said, patting my shoulder. 'You'll get it in time.'

He sat at his workbench, on a stool which looked as though he might have made it himself long ago. Then he

pulled a smaller stool out from beneath the bench. He motioned for me to sit beside him.

I sat.

'Some of the tools are extremely sharp,' he said. 'You must be careful.' I knew from the tone of his voice that he really meant this.

I watched and listened as Mr Silver showed me chisels, gouges and files, told of their uses and taught me how to use each of them. He taught me about different types of wood, of their advantages and disadvantages. He spoke of carving as though it woke something in him. I'd had no idea that Mr Silver was into this so much, like Pete was about football or one of our cousins was about fast cars that he couldn't afford, but I soon realised that this was Mr Silver's passion.

The summer wore on and I practised. I learnt. At first, I'd expected that he'd just show me how to carve – I'd thought that was all there was to know – but he taught me how I needed to appreciate something, to know it, before I even began to carve it, like he had with that mallard those few years earlier. He explained the importance of it all, of how it was down to me, my imagination and my hands, to create something that would last a lifetime and might really mean something to someone. He was a natural teacher, even though he'd spent his working life on the railways. He was patient, explained everything with big stories that had endings which answered my questions.

It occurred to me, one afternoon in the workshop, to ask him a different kind of question. 'Who taught *you* all of this, Mr Silver?'

For a few seconds, his mind was elsewhere. 'My father

taught me this,' he said. There was pride in his words. I knew this had huge meaning for Mr Silver, and in some way I understood why, but then my heart sank when I thought of my own dad, whose main lesson to me had been that someone can leave you forever at any time and without warning. 'And now I'm here to pass it all onto you,' Mr Silver said.

It was that night, as I lay in bed and thought back to that conversation, when I realised something. Instead of a wooden mallard, perhaps it had been this knowledge of carving, this skill, that'd been Mr Silver's intended gift for me two Christmases before. Maybe he'd known I'd one day knock on his door and ask for it.

I changed over those months. Mum said it was the summer I became a man. While Mr Silver had been teaching his gift, the summer passed by, and it was an early autumn day when I went to his workshop after school and saw a piece of lime wood on the bench. It was a bit bigger than the pieces we'd usually worked with.

'I got it for you,' he said.

'Thank you.' I picked it up, was delighted with it. I felt excited by the opportunity to bring something into existence.

'What will you create?' he asked.

I looked to the pictures of ideas that we'd been collecting from newspapers and magazines and had stuck on the wall in his workshop. There were animals, trees, faces, buildings even. I had lots to choose from, but then I remembered back to that morning when I'd seen something, really early, when the estate was still and nearly dark, as I'd been doing my paper round. Something had

caught my attention, on a fence near the ditch, and I'd been stunned when I realised I was being watched. 'An owl,' I said.

Mr Silver smiled.

I chipped and chiselled, and I concentrated, and for weeks I didn't hang around with the other boys or go to the community centre. Pete was getting annoyed at me for all the time I wasn't around, but at least he had football practice to go to, and he'd ride his skateboard with his mates on the estate. Under Mr Silver's watch, his guidance and advice, the lump of wood became roughly egg-shaped. Then feet appeared on a branch. Folded wings. Slowly, the owl hatched, with its heart-face and round eyes. I'd never been so proud of anything in all my life, and I told Mr Silver so.

'Give it to your mum, as a gift,' he suggested.

And I did.

7th December

Spencer and I are in the gym locker room, following an after-work session. He got a different job a few months back, his new office just down the road from mine, which is handy for us meeting up.

'I bought Daisy-May this cute bracelet-making thing when I went Christmas shopping the other day.'

'Ah,' Spencer says, pulling his T-shirt on. 'She'll love that.'

'I thought she might.'

'Only a few weeks away now, isn't it?'

'Two weeks Sunday,' I say.

'We're going to Joanne's parents this year.'

'Are you?' I'm jarred for a moment. I'd thought – perhaps a bit presumptuously, I realise now – that with Mum and Ricardo being away, I'd be at Spencer's.

'Staying there Christmas Eve, so they get to have Christmas morning to open presents with Daisy. We're having dinner with them and coming home in the evening.'

'That'll be lovely,' I say.

'You going to your mum's?'

'She'll be away. Three weeks in Australia, with Ricardo.'

'She's living the high life these days.'

'I know,' I say, pleased for her. After Dad left, Mum didn't do much other than work and look after me and Pete as we grew up. 'Is it OK if I borrow your car, to take them to the airport?'

'Yeah, absolutely.'

'Thanks. They were planning on a taxi, but I'd quite like to see them off.'

Spencer is crouching, tying the laces on his trainers, but he pauses and looks up at me. 'So if they're away, what are you gonna do for Christmas?'

I sweep my hand through my hair a couple of times; it's still damp from the shower. 'Might just be a quiet one this year.'

'Come to our place Christmas evening and stay over.'

I shake my head. 'You'll be knackered. And it'll be good for just the three of you to have some family time.'

Spencer shrugs. 'You *are* family, Dan.'

I don't know what to say. I slide my jacket on. 'How about Boxing Day?'

He stands, pulls his baseball cap over his head. 'All right then, if you're not gonna budge. We'll have a Christmas Day with you… on Boxing Day.'

'Sounds good,' I say. And it really does.

It's cold and dark as we leave the gym.

Spencer shines the torch from his phone, so I can see to undo my bike lock. Just as I'm putting the chain in my bag, I notice Amber coming in our direction, her shoes clip-clopping on the footpath. 'Oh no,' I mutter, 'it's her again,' as though she's someone I don't want to see, which isn't the case at all.

'Who?'

'Don't look, Spence!' I whisper.

'Who's she?' He turns back to me, his torch blinding my eyes.

I squint, nudge his hand away. 'She lives in my block.'

'You fancy her!'

'Shh!'

Amber is about to go past us. I'm trying to fasten my bag, a suddenly complicated thing to do, and although I don't plan to look up, just as she passes by, I do exactly that.

'Hi,' she says.

'Hi,' I say.

Spencer and I watch her walk away. Her winter coat is silver-grey. Her scarf is light blue. I'm a little stunned; I didn't think she'd remember us meeting at all.

Spencer prods me with his elbow. 'She likes you.'

'She does not,' I say, thinking the idea ridiculous, or at least very unlikely. 'She just said hi to be polite.'

'Yeah, but she smiled at you in *that* way.'

'That wasn't a smile, mate. That was a smirk. She thinks we're a pair of clowns.'

Spencer laughs. 'Seriously though, Dan. It's been a long time since, y'know, you know who. It's time you met someone again.'

I try to give Spencer a look that tells him I don't want to have this conversation, which makes him grin and roll his eyes. 'See you later,' I say, getting onto my bike.

'See ya.'

I switch my bike lights on, and set off.

It's not long before I see Amber up ahead. She's heading towards the estate. I don't want to cycle past her, so I turn off of my usual route and go down a side street.

I know every shortcut around here, every back alley, quick routes between rows of garages and through playgrounds. I stop pedalling, let my bike run, and only when the momentum is nearly gone do I begin again,

slowly. I don't want to reach the flats before her, to wait for the lift, which sometimes takes forever to arrive when called, and risk seeing her there. The idea of being in the lift together, after she might possibly have heard Spencer saying – a little loudly – about me fancying her, fills me with dread. Yet seeing her again tonight has somehow made my evening, my whole day, better, even though I'm a bit disappointed at myself for thinking so desperately. I don't know why I'm being like this at times lately, somewhat unsettled. A little confused, even. I've been having a weird feeling, as though something very good or very bad is going to happen.

I take my time. Some roads are busy with cars. A crowd of kids hang out at the bus stop. Warmly dressed people stand outside the Queen's Head with drinks in their hands. The backstreets are quiet, mine, as I ride through pools of light from lampposts. I'm orbiting the estate, keep glancing towards my distant tower block and the identical one that stands beside it, a parallel universe.

I let go of the handlebar and lean back on the saddle. I'd often ride my bike with no hands when I was young. I smile as I think back to those good times, to Mum always telling me off for doing this no-hands thing, saying I'd fall off and hurt myself one day.

Firsts

I was riding my bike around the estate on an afternoon owned by the sun – it was the summer I'd left school. The green was busy. A father and son were chasing each other with water pistols. Some girls were jumping a skipping rope. People were sunbathing on chairs and picnic blankets. Boys were having a five-a-side, Pete amongst them, their T-shirts on the grass as goal posts.

I dropped my bike on the front lawn and went inside, the door on the latch the way it always was during the day when Pete and I were in and out. The hallway seemed dark in contrast to the brightness outside. I was dizzy for a moment until my eyes adjusted. I went to the kitchen and was about to get an ice lolly, when the phone started ringing. Through the window, I saw Mum hanging washing in the back garden, so I closed the freezer door and went to the phone.

'Hello?'

'Could I speak to Daniel, please?'

'I'm Daniel,' I said, surprised the call was for me because it never usually was. Hearing the woman's voice, I wondered which of my friends' mums it was.

'It's Jenny, from the recruitment agency.'

Three weeks earlier, I'd had my first ever job interview. I'd waited every day for a phone call, checked the mat every morning for a letter. Then I'd given up, had known anyway I wouldn't be good enough to be the one they picked. 'Oh, right,' I said.

'I've just heard back on your interview. I'm pleased to tell you they've offered you the job.'

I can't remember another word of that conversation, but at some point I took a pen from the jar on the phone table, opened the notepad that was always there and wrote *9am Monday* onto a blank page.

After the call, I stood there for a moment, my world fuzzy like when I'd come inside from dazzling sunlight.

Then I ran through the house. '*Mum!*' She was pegging some jeans onto the line as I stepped into the garden. 'I got the job.'

'I knew you would!' She shook her fists in the air as the jeans fell to the ground.

I ran to Mr Silver's house to tell him, then rode my bike across the green to tell Pete too. In celebration, Mum made my favourite dinner that night: sausages, homemade chips and fried egg.

The next day, we went shopping. Mum bought me a pair of black trousers, three shirts, two ties. She decided my school shoes would do, even though they were scuffed. I really wanted new shoes, though I didn't say so, as when we'd chosen the clothes, I'd seen her checking the price tags, while trying to appear that she wasn't.

I couldn't sleep the night before my first day. As I lay awake I could see my white shirt in the darkness, like a ghost of the future hanging on the wardrobe door handle, while in the bunk above me Pete slept soundly. It would also be his first day back at school after the summer holidays.

The following morning, Mum kissed us both goodbye at the doorstep. Pete, who was nearly as tall as me by then,

wore his school uniform and I my new outfit, with the tie that'd taken me countless attempts to get just right. I'd spent a lot of time combing my hair.

'I'm coming to the bus stop with you,' Pete said, as we walked down the path.

'But school's the other way.'

'I know.'

I was glad of the company.

'Are you nervous?'

'Not really,' I said, though I knew Pete had clocked that I'd barely touched my cereal. I never liked to admit any kind of weakness to Pete, not since Dad left. I thought it important to always tell him that everything was absolutely fine, and that there was nothing in the world to worry about.

We crossed the green, and when we reached the main road at the edge of the estate we sat on the bench at the bus stop, the wooden one with names and stick people and swear words etched into it.

Pete opened his school bag, took out his lunchbox and handed me a mini chocolate bar. 'Take it,' he said.

'It's all right, Pete. Mum's put one in mine, too.'

'You'll need it more. You'll be *working*,' he said. He looked at me quite seriously.

I took the bar from him, the contents of the wrapper now more valuable than chocolate. 'Thanks, Pete.' I opened my bag and my lunchbox, and put it alongside the cheese sandwich Mum had made, the apple, and my own mini chocolate bar.

More people gathered at the bus stop. I counted my coins again, to check I had enough for the fare. I glanced at

my watch, as although I had plenty of time, I was dreading I'd be late. I worried, thinking that I didn't know how to talk to people who worked in an office, wondered whether I could really do the job, and even worse whether they'd got their phone numbers mixed up and given it to the wrong applicant. Then, Pete tapped me on the arm.

'Bus is coming,' he said, and we both stood.

'See you tonight, Pete.'

'Good luck, Dan the Man,' he said.

I paid the driver, then took the ticket from the machine. As the bus pulled away I settled on the back seat, turned and looked through the rear window.

Pete was waving.

I waved back.

I arrived at the office a bit early. After thinking about whether I should wait outside until the last minute, or go straight in, I pushed the bar of the revolving glass doors into the reception area with posh chairs, massive plants and a smell of coffee. I went to the front desk; the same lady I'd seen here when I'd had my interview.

'You can wait over there,' she said kindly. 'They'll be with you shortly.'

There were others waiting. I sat beside a boy of a similar age to me who looked as nervous as I felt.

After a moment of silence, he whispered, 'Is it your first day too?'

I nodded.

He exhaled with relief, then held his hand towards me, to shake. 'I'm Spencer.'

Over the following weeks I absorbed my new environment. I went from amongst the oldest at school to the youngest at work. I learned the things I was expected to do and the things I shouldn't do, got to know the people who were chatty and discovered some grumpy ones to be avoided. I learned how to file, how to fax. When the phone rang, it was my job to answer it politely.

I'd meet Spencer, who was working on a different floor to me, at lunchtimes. We even met at weekends, mostly to ride our bikes or go swimming, and I took Pete along too, so he didn't feel left out. There was one subject that dominated mine and Spencer's conversations: payday. We counted down the days to our first. I'd got Mum to go into the bank with me to open a savings account, ready, though I also planned how I'd spend some of my pay. When it finally arrived, Spencer and I went shopping in town after work.

It was getting dark by the time I got home. Mum was cooking dinner. I knew Pete was at home too, as there was loud music coming from our bedroom. Pete had become a fan of 2 Unlimited, and I think half the estate could tell that he liked their new record a lot.

I put my shopping bags on the table, then kissed Mum's cheek.

'How was work?'

'Good, thanks,' I said. I slid my wallet from my pocket and took out the notes I'd withdrawn from the bank: housekeeping for Mum. We'd had several discussions over the previous weeks, Mum saying I didn't need to start paying anything yet as I was too young, me arguing that I wasn't.

Seeing the cash in my hand, she waved it away.

From my carrier bag, I took out the sweets I'd bought her.

'Oh lovely!' she said. 'I won't say no to those.' She opened the box and put a sweet in her mouth, before putting the oven gloves on to take out a tray of fish fingers.

I leaned against the sideboard and watched, having long, long learned my lesson not to interfere with dinner. She scraped a curl of butter, dropped it into a saucepan of drained potatoes then began to mash them. With fish fingers and mash, I knew without looking that the other pan contained peas.

I realised I still held the notes. 'I'll leave the housekeeping on top of the bread bin, then.'

'No you won't!' she said.

But I did. 'Pete!' I called, before Mum had a chance to argue. The music coming from our bedroom was still loud and I could hear the rhythmic creaking of floorboards above my head: Pete dancing. I went to the foot of the stairs. '*Pete!*'

The music stopped. He came bounding down, then into the kitchen where I handed him his present.

'No way,' he said, recognising the logo on the box. He opened the lid and pulled the tissue paper aside, revealing the trainers he'd been going on about for months, that he wanted so badly, that all the other kids on the estate were talking about.

'Oh, Dan the Man!' He dropped the trainers to the floor and twisted his feet into them. 'Amazing!'

I took the last item out of the shopping bag: a bottle of sherry.

Mum raised her eyebrows. 'How did you get served that?' she asked, then the kitchen was filled with the sound of her banging the masher onto the side of the saucepan.

'Spencer went into the shop for me, he looks older.'

Mum rolled her eyes. 'Mr S will be delighted.'

I went round to Mr Silver's house and knocked on his front door hard, as sometimes his hearing wasn't so good. Then I gave him a long while to answer, because I knew it took time for him to rise from his armchair. Through the frosted glass, I saw him making progress along the hall.

'Hello, Daniel,' he said, when he opened the door.

'Hi, Mr Silver.'

'Come on in.'

'I'd better not,' I said. 'Mum's just dishing-up. But I wanted to give you this.' I held the bottle out to him.

'For me?'

'I thought you might like it.' The bottle passed from my hands to his. 'It's my first payday today, you see, from that job I got.'

It was a moment before he said, 'And you bought this for me, from your first pay packet?'

'I did.'

He considered the bottle, as though he was seeing the label for the first time, even though I knew he had a little glass of this brand once in a while and had done for all the years we'd been his neighbour, since I was just a baby. When he looked back up, his eyes seemed a bit watery. 'It's the best gift I've ever received.'

9th December

Norman from Customer Services has just arrived at the office and is approaching our bank of desks. I already know what he's going to say.

'What've you been doing to yourself, then?' As he takes his seat, he's eyeing my face with fascination and not an ounce of concern.

The graze on my chin and the bruise across my cheek are quite noticeable, though fortunately he can't see, beneath my shirt, my sore shoulder and scraped elbow. 'I fell off my bike on my way home from the gym the other night.'

'How did you manage that?'

I think for a moment. 'It was dark,' I say, which is not untrue, though it isn't the reason I fell off either. Norman, who is astute to anything withheld, like a small bird to the tiniest of sounds, has sensed this. Luckily, Marie breaks the moment by bringing our morning drinks. A packet of digestives are on the tray too, opened. I bet she started them while she was waiting for the kettle to boil. 'Lovely, thanks,' I say, taking my tea.

We all have our own mug: Marie's has a vintage design of flowers, mine is plain duck-egg blue and Norman's has the logo of a chocolate brand and no doubt came with an Easter egg from his kids. We settle back at our desks, more peacefully with the relaxing mood that a steaming cup and a crumbly biscuit brings. The immense spreadsheet on my computer screen seems a little bit less dire now.

'What are we all up to this weekend?' Marie asks. She blows on her coffee.

'Swimming class first thing tomorrow,' Norman says. 'Dance class in the afternoon.'

Nathaniel from Marketing peers over the desk divider. 'I never had you down for a dancer, Norman?'

We all know that the swimming and dancing is for his youngest daughter rather than for Norman. He's just a driver. But Nathaniel is obviously bored and on the wind-up.

'For my daughter,' Norman says firmly, before looking to me and rolling his eyes.

Catching Nathaniel's smirk before he ducks his head back down, I try to keep a straight face.

'The girls have swimming tomorrow, too,' Marie says. 'We'll see you there.'

Norman raises his eyebrows and nods. He can't speak, as his mouth is full of biscuit now.

Marie turns in her swivel chair. 'Dan?'

'Football practice tonight.'

'Of course,' she says, knowing my schedule for leading football practice and the other things I volunteer for at the community centre on the estate. 'It's Friday.'

'You've just reminded me,' I say. 'I need to send an email for the bake sale. The proceeds for the community centre were pretty good last year.'

'Go for it.'

I type an email, then send it to the whole office, telling them that the date of the event is 21st December and that donations of their homemade baking or their shop-bought contributions are very welcome. Then I search my desktop

for the poster from last year, and update it. I print it, and Tim the office junior, who's very hungover this morning and not capable of anything remotely complicated, gives me a hand taping the posters up in the kitchen, on the noticeboard, in Reception, on the doors to the toilets. Everywhere, so that when bake sale day comes, none of them can use the excuse that they didn't know about it.

The day passes quickly, as they often do at work as we're all so busy. When it's nearly five I pack up, then quickly get changed for cycling. As I'm leaving, I notice that the stinky elf hat has changed coat hooks; someone has tried it on. I'm satisfied at seeing this, at knowing that someone couldn't resist. I'm still smiling as I pass through Reception. 'Have a nice evening,' I call, and though the receptionist doesn't look up, she sort of raises her hand.

I ride back to the estate – darkness and car lights, buses and puddles – and all the way I keep both hands on the handlebar.

At the community centre, I set up for football practice. Ball games on the green haven't been allowed for years, such freedoms a thing of the past, so the kids now are even more grateful than we were for the small indoor pitch here. I've led the under-sixteen's football on Friday nights since I was eighteen. Half my life. On other nights, I help at bingo and the book club and whatever else might be going on. I enjoy giving something back to this place that Pete and I appreciated when we were young.

The session goes quickly, noisily as always, with the sound of footballers shouting, me shouting, my whistle bouncing piercingly off the walls. An argument between

two boys is forgotten after they shake hands. There's laughter and chatter as we cool down with drinks served by Sanjay, another volunteer. By seven thirty the kids are on their way out the door and I'm locking up to calls of *thanks, Dan* as they all head back to their homes, to the rows of terraced houses and blocks of flats on the estate.

I'm chilly wearing my shorts as I push my bike across the green towards Mum's. I always go home after football on Fridays. We see each other here and there at other points of the week, but this is our main catch-up. I know she'll have dinner ready.

There's an enormous sense of belonging that I feel, always feel, as I slide my key into the lock, open the door and step into the house that I grew up in. It's warm here tonight, smells wonderfully of cooking and of the vanilla air freshener that sits on the console table in the hall; the table that, many years ago, Mum had fallen in love with at a second-hand shop and Pete and I had carried all the way home.

'What have you done to your face?' Mum looks very concerned, as though I've just walked into the kitchen actually gushing blood.

'I fell off my bike the other day.'

'Oh, Dan!'

'It's just a bruise.'

'And a graze.'

I kiss Mum's cheek.

'How was work?' she asks, as I sit down.

'It was all right.' I never have much to tell her. Sometimes it feels as though I've nothing going on in life other than work, volunteering, the gym, and of course my

wood carvings. 'I'm working on a new carving.'

Mum carries a square dish of steaming pasta bake to the dining table. She places it alongside a big bowl of green leaves, cucumber, tomato and hoops of red onion. She sits opposite me, tucking her chair in. 'What's it of?'

'A fox,' I say, as I serve the food onto Mum's plate, then my own.

'That sounds nice.'

'I've seen one a few times on the estate recently,' I say. 'Beautiful it is.' I blow onto a forkful, eat it eagerly. 'You make the best pasta bake in the world, Mum.'

She grins, lifts her hand and waves the compliment away.

The ticking of the kitchen clock and the scraping of cutlery on plates are the only sounds for a while.

'Have you spoken to Pete?'

'He called yesterday,' Mum says. 'Owen wanted to tell me about a painting he'd done at school that'd won best in the class.'

I can imagine his little face, his excitement at hearing that he'd won. 'That's great.'

Mum smiles and nods.

'I'll give them a ring soon.' It feels odd sometimes to talk of Pete in this house when he's so far away. I'm happy for him and Camille and the nice life they have in Canada, but there's a gaping hole here, in this meal and moment, without Pete's voice and his sprightly presence. I try not to think about it. 'Looking forward to your holiday?'

'Very much so,' she says. 'We went shopping for it the other day and I bought a few new outfits, a hat, and Ricardo got sunglasses.'

'You're gonna have a great time.'

Mum giggles, but then her expression becomes more serious, as if she's remembered something not so good. 'You *are* going to Spencer's for Christmas, right?'

I could never lie to Mum, though I can't exactly tell her I'm on my own for Christmas, as she might cancel her holiday. My foot is bouncing on the floor beneath the table as I struggle to think of a way out of the situation, then Ricardo arrives home, sweeping the conversation away as Mum stands to get another plate from the cupboard.

'Dan,' he says, putting his hand on my shoulder as he passes by. 'Good to see you.'

'You too, Ric.'

He kisses Mum.

I fill his plate.

He sits, and the three of us finish our dinner, followed by apple pie and custard, all the while talking about my day, of Mum's day, and Ricardo – this later addition to our family, but now it feels like he's always been here – he tells us of his day, too.

'And how was your football coaching tonight?' he asks. He speaks posher than my family – every now and then, I still notice it.

'Good. Lively as ever. Feels like it's been a long day though, what with work as well.'

'Those kids are lucky to have you, Dan,' Mum says.

'There are other volunteers too. Fiona and Sanjay are there a couple of nights a week at least.'

'No one gives more of their time than you do.'

The Volunteer

I was on my way to meet Spencer for a drink – we were only just old enough to get served – when I saw Pete along with a few others standing outside the community centre. The metal shutters were down, a big padlock fastened at the bottom.

'They late opening?' I asked.

'Look at the sign.' Pete motioned to the shutter, where I saw a sheet of paper attached by sticky tape. I moved closer until I could read the words written in black marker: CLOSED INDEFINITELY.

'Because there's no volunteers,' a voice behind me said.

I turned and saw Mr Silver. I hadn't noticed him there. He was sitting on the little seat of his walking frame, taking a rest. He'd started doing a circuit of the green each evening, to keep his joints moving. I wandered over to him. 'What happened to David?' David had led football practice for as long as I could remember.

'Left in a hurry. Some trouble with the police, apparently. I'm surprised you haven't heard. The whole estate knows.'

David was widely respected for his efforts at the community centre, though I wasn't shocked at this news. None of us knew what he did for work, even though he wore loads of jewellery and was one of the few people on the estate who owned a flash car.

'And Barbara?' Barbara ran the book club and served the refreshments on football nights.

'She got a swap. Moved to some place miles away, to live closer to her sister.'

That was two-thirds of the volunteers gone. 'What about old Eddie?' Eddie had been calling bingo numbers every Wednesday night since before I was born.

'Died.'

'He never!'

'True!' Mr Silver said. 'They did a lovely spread for him at the Queen's Head.'

Mr Silver had a warm expression, though I wasn't sure if his thoughts were with memories of Eddie, or those sandwiches.

I was sorry to hear about his passing, and realised that I was a bit detached from these goings-on of the estate, what with being at work all week and going places with Spencer at the weekends. At eighteen, I was no longer going to football myself, though I used to look forward to it for the laughs and the camaraderie, for the getting out of the house where Pete and I would sometimes ache with boredom. I knew how it was to grow up on the estate with so little to do, even though I had my carvings. The community centre had saved us, especially after Dad left. It'd been a distraction. 'What are the kids going to do now?'

'You could always volunteer yourself,' Mr Silver said.

For weeks, there'd been a note on the window saying VOLUNTEERS NEEDED. Every time I'd seen it, I'd walked straight past it. 'Where would I even start with that? The place is closed already.'

As if he'd already considered this problem, he said, 'You could start by knocking on the door of Barbara's old

flat. Ask the new tenant for the address of the place she's swapped to. Write Barbara a note.'

I thought about this. 'I'd love to volunteer, really I would, but it's not just about work here though, is it?'

'How so?'

'Like Barbara, and David and Eddie come to think of it. Loads of times I've seen them listening to people's problems or trying to cheer them up. Trying to sort things out for folks who need help. Takes a specific kind of person to be able to do all that stuff, and that isn't me.'

'I totally disagree.'

I thought about it a moment longer. 'I'd be no good at it at all.'

Mr Silver sighed. Standing unsteadily, he gripped his walking frame, our conversation apparently over. 'Take care, Daniel.'

'Bye, Mr Silver.' I watched him slowly walk away, then I went back over to Pete and to the others with him. One of the girls, whose name I didn't know, was chewing gum, her arms folded as she stared across the green. Pete's best mate, Terry, was holding a cigarette behind his back to hide it from me, which was a bit pointless as with the billowing smoke it just looked like his backside was on fire. I remembered then: a couple of nights previous, I'd thought Pete had come home smelling of smoke, and that was very unlike him because his behaviour was always good. Well, good-ish.

Pete looked dejected. He loved football practice. 'We might as well go.'

'Yeah,' a girl said.

A feeling of disappointment hung in the air. I couldn't

bear it.

'The one bloody thing we have to look forward to all week,' she said, smacking the shutter just hard enough that it rattled and made her point.

The group began to disperse. My eyes were on Terry, who, along with Pete and those girls, was heading towards the swings. 'Terry,' I called.

He turned to me.

'If I find out that you're encouraging my little brother to smoke, then you and me are gonna fall out. Understood?'

He cleared his throat. 'Understood, Dan.'

'Good.' I didn't look at Pete and instead began making my way across the green. I knew that he'd shout at me later when he got home, for embarrassing him in front of those girls, but I wasn't too worried about that.

I carried on my way to the Queen's Head, to meet Spencer for that drink.

I was baffled when I received a letter in the post from Barbara a week later, saying she was delighted to hear that I'd volunteered to take over the community centre. She went on to tell where light switches and heating controls were, where the fuse box was, where things were stored. Enclosed was a key for the shutter padlock. She signed her note off with, *Good luck, Dan.*

I didn't know for sure how news of my apparent volunteering had found its way to Barbara, though I had my suspicions. However, with the key in my hand I was nervously pleased at the prospect of reopening the community centre. I knew it would need a team effort, the

way it always had, so I began to ask around. Fiona, who lived in one of the tower blocks, said she'd be happy to become a regular volunteer, as did Sanjay, who lived three doors down from us and had been in the year above me at school.

It wasn't long before the three of us had reopened the centre with me leading football practice, which Pete found hilarious as I've never been any good at football. Bingo night and book club started again. Sanjay arranged new exercise mornings for Saturdays. Other volunteers joined, and along with them came new ideas and activities: netball, quiz nights, dart nights, a table tennis tournament, board game sessions, which proved to be great for bringing different generations together. I somehow became manager of the community centre and in this felt a sense of purpose, one which I hadn't actually realised I was missing before.

It wasn't until a month or so later that I found time to go to Mr Silver's for tea and a catch-up. We were in his living room. I'd just updated him on what'd been happening at the community centre, of all the things we were planning and of how I'd settled into this new role better than I'd expected to. It was then that I remembered the letter from Barbara, and that someone had told her the untruth that I'd volunteered. 'Would you happen to know how that found its way to Barbara?'

'I wouldn't know anything about that, Daniel,' he said, and he turned to look out of the window.

I smiled, having spotted the first and only fib Mr Silver ever told me.

11th December

Spencer has been held up and sent a text to say he won't make it to gym this afternoon. I'm bored as I rest between sets. The gym is pretty empty, as it often is on Sundays.

There are only a couple of Christmas decorations up here, along with an artificial tree in the reception area. Beneath it are wrapped parcels tied with ribbon. They're all the same size and shape and I suspect they might be empty protein bar boxes.

I do another set on the bench press.

Resting, I look at the red foil garland that's dangling from the ceiling and think that I'll put my decorations up at home tonight. I've more reason than ever to make an effort this year, on my own, to not let Christmas pass me by. It might be all right, this spending it alone thing. I'll get plenty of food in. I can watch whatever movies I want. Might as well make myself a turkey roast – it's only once a year. A pudding and cream, too. It'll be fine, I think, but as I stroll over to the pull-up bars, I wonder how much flights to Canada are. It'd be brilliant to visit Pete, Camille and Owen for the festivities, but then I remember I really can't afford it. There's stuff I need money for in the new year, repairs in the flat, and I need to put some cash aside as the boiler's been threatening to give up.

I begin my pull-ups. So me it is this year then, just me. And who knows, it really might be all right. It might be fun. I'm not sure I believe myself on this, though.

On the way home I stop at the supermarket. I pick a

box which has fifty cards, ten each of five traditional designs: Father Christmas trudging through snow, sack slung over his shoulder. An open, roaring fireplace with stockings hanging on the mantel. Holly, with deep green leaves dusted with frost and plentiful red berries. A snowman with a carrot nose and coal eyes. The last design is a nativity scene. I open them to check the quality of the card, then scan the writing on the back of the box. Satisfied to read that a portion of profits are to go to charity, I put the cards into my basket, then a second box of the same.

It's cold outside tonight, but my flat is warm. There were six envelopes on the doormat when I got home, cards for me from people around the estate, which I've put up on the shelf in the living room. I've eaten a good meal, just made myself a hot chocolate and have picked some Christmas music. On my little kitchen table is a notepad and pen, my address book and the two boxes of cards I bought.

I list the names of those at work, starting with the receptionist and working my way through the office in my mind. Many cards get exchanged in the office. A few years back, one of them told me this only happens because I instigate it, seeming only half-pleased, which made me smile.

People from the estate are next on the list. Some are more recent arrivals that I've met, though many I've known since I was young. My mind goes to Amber, to the brief conversation we had because of the post mix-up, then seeing her in town and outside the gym. I'd love to write her a card. *To Amber, Merry Christmas, from Daniel, Flat 157.*

But I can't. She might find it weird, and she'd probably be correct.

I write the names of those further afield: a few school friends who moved; our way of knowing the other is all right is by our yearly cards. An old work colleague, who traditionally sends me one and I traditionally send one back. A girl who I went out with briefly in my teenage years, who I sort of stayed in touch with.

With my blue pen I write words of best wishes as my festive music plays. The number of cards I write gets a bit higher every year, though unfortunately a name or two comes off the list each year, too: those we have sadly lost. In this, my thirty-fourth Christmas, my list stretches to just over one hundred people. I only realise this when I run out of cards. I remember I have a few left from last year, and after searching through my drawers I find them. They have a picture of a robin, the plump bird sitting on a bare winter branch.

I address the envelopes for those to be posted and pile them separately to the ones for work. In another pile are those to be hand-delivered on the estate, in the correct order for the route I'll take later.

The big cardboard box of decorations, which I'd taken from the cupboard earlier, is in the living room. I pull it in front of the sofa and sit as I begin to dig through it. There's a smaller box inside which has baubles wrapped in newspaper – I think of which night after work might be best for me to buy a tree. I find other decorations, the garlands, the mobiles, the lights on green wire wrapped around like a bird's nest. There's a snow globe with Father Christmas inside. I shake it, then watch as the flakes settle.

Taking the rest of the decorations out, I wonder, is there really any point in me putting all these up, or buying the tree, if there's only going to be me here? My initial thought is yes, but as I consider it more, my excitement of putting the decs up is fading. There really is no point. I stuff everything back into the box. As I return it to the cupboard, I try to see the positive in that at least I'm going to save twenty-odd quid on a tree that I won't be buying.

In the hall I pull my jacket on, my scarf, woollen hat. I make my way down through the tower, taking the stairs and walking the landings where I have cards to put through letterboxes, quietly, as it's a bit late. Reaching the ground floor, I go out onto the estate. It's very cold now. After delivering to the other tower, I walk along the rows of terraced houses, posting, posting.

My hands are empty as I head home. The estate is silent, deserted. Too chilly perhaps for the older teenagers who usually gather in small groups and sit in the kid's playground, too late for the evening dog walkers and joggers. I'm approaching the green when I realise I'm not alone after all: the fox glances at me twice as it crosses my path. I try to get a good look at its bushy tail – that's going to be the most challenging part of my wood carving – but then it's gone.

Back in the flat, I quickly iron my work shirts for the week ahead, wishing now, as always, that I hadn't left it until Sunday night. I brush my teeth, then switch lights off as I go from room to room.

I lie in bed and try to find sleep, but with my mind refusing to switch off the way it has been lately, I realise that it's two weeks today until Christmas. It'll be the first

since I moved into this flat that I've not put those decorations up.

Flat 157

I was still young when I bought it, though it felt as if I'd been saving the deposit for a hundred years. Living with Mum and Pete, our bills divided by three, I was able to put a little bit away each month – that's how it started. I worked my usual job on weekdays, and then I got another, a weekend job as a barman, so that I could save more. On top of that, I volunteered. Every day I was exhausted. Mum told me that I didn't need to work so many hours, that I could live at home for years more, or forever, but getting my own place was something I wanted to do, especially after Pete moved out. The bedroom we'd shared for so long was suddenly very quiet, the bunk above me empty. But Pete was not alone.

It was on a summer evening that I first heard of Camille, when Pete and I were walking home across the green.

'I've met someone,' he said.

His few choice words, his avoidance of eye contact, stood out. We always spoke openly about girlfriends, but something was different. I somehow knew not to ask where he'd met her, or if they'd slept together yet, or any of the other usual stuff. Instead, I asked, 'Do you think she might be the one you stay together with forever?'

After a moment, Pete nodded. 'I hope so.'

We were approaching the house. I nudged Pete with my elbow, which made him stumble and giggle. 'Better tell Mum, then,' I said.

That night, over dinner, he did just that.

And it was at our kitchen table a few days later that Mum and I met Camille for the first time, when she came for a meal.

We liked her. Unlike Pete's previous relationships, it was clear they were a brilliant match, each as lively as the other, already a team. It was no surprise when they announced their engagement. It wasn't long after that Spencer met Joanne, who in time would become almost as much of a friend to me as Spencer himself. They, too, got engaged.

A couple of years later, a slightly more unexpected addition came into our little group: Ricardo. After raising me and Pete, during which she never allowed much time for herself, Mum was socialising more than she used to. She'd have a drink with people from work, took up exercising and went on speed walks around the estate with one of the neighbours. She had a friend that she went to see a film with once in a while. She'd been single for so long, since Dad left, yet one night, there at the cinema, after their fifty-something years on the planet living their different lives, Mum and Ricardo were standing beside one another in the queue for popcorn. Their eyes met, apparently.

Pete and I were keen to meet him, to check him out just like Mum did when we'd met new girlfriends, and we knew right away we had nothing to worry about with Ricardo. We really liked the way he was around Mum. He styled his grey hair young for his years – shaved at the sides, spikey on top – and he dressed a bit trendy. He had a playful attitude that matched Mum's.

While everyone else's life was passing through these changes, mine stayed much the same, but I saved. I went out less, cancelled my gym membership for a while and used the park instead. My only big spend was learning to drive, but after I passed my test I didn't buy a car. I preferred my bike anyway.

My savings grew. The tens turned into hundreds, which turned into thousands. I researched mortgages, asked people for advice, and saved, saved. Then, finally, one day I got my keys. It was flat 157, on the fifteenth floor of one of the two towers on the estate, only a few minutes' walk from home.

Mum and Ricardo, Pete and Camille, Spencer and Joanne all helped on moving-in day. I didn't have much to move though, so they were more there for the event, for the support. I was so broke from the deposit that I couldn't even afford a bed, and initially I was to be sleeping on a mattress. There was no sofa. Spencer and Joanne bought me saucepans as a moving-in present. The work crowd clubbed together and got me a crockery set. Mum had bags full of things that I hadn't even thought of: tea towels, a tin opener, cleaning products, and as soon as we got into the flat she had a tape measure at the windows for the curtains she was determined to buy.

When everyone had left that evening, it sank in: I was living on my own. I hadn't pictured it this way. A part of me felt as though I was missing something by not sharing the moment with someone special, but rather than ruining my mood, the thought was only in the back of my mind, detached, like a conversation I was overhearing. Besides, I didn't expect to be living there alone forever.

I went out onto my new balcony. I took a deep breath of evening air and for the first time appreciated my new view of the estate far below, of the hundreds of rooftops, the strip of tall trees and bushes alongside the ditch. I could just about see the house I'd moved out of beyond the green, where I'd grown up with Mum and Pete, and Dad before he'd left. Where Mum still lived, and Ricardo soon would. My gaze went to the house next door, where dear old Mr Silver was probably spending his evening alone, too.

13th December

Tuesday morning. I'm off work. I have tomorrow booked off too, using up the last of my annual leave before I lose it at the end of the year. I have that luxurious feeling right now of having just got up an hour later than usual, lazing about the flat and sipping a coffee when it sort of feels like I should be in the office.

I take the four envelopes from the doormat, then go to the living room. Always nice, getting cards. Three are from people who live on the estate, and the other, with a cute picture of a snow-covered cottage, from someone who moved away. I find space for them with the other cards on top of the cabinet.

In the box room, I settle at my workbench. The piece of lime wood, or, rather, the fox, doesn't look like much so far. I hold the lumpy, half-formed thing in my left hand, and in my right, a gouge. Though I've only seen that fox out on the estate while it's walking, I'm creating this carving with it sitting, its tail wrapped around its front legs to form part of the base. I've decided to size it small enough to sit on a shelf, but big enough to be the centre of attention there.

Today, I focus my efforts on the shape of its back and its hind legs, though all the while I'm considering how I might fashion the snout, ears, wonder whether its head should be straight or tilted. I'm about to look through my books for some fox pictures for inspiration, but decide not to; it's *that* fox I want to carve, to recreate. I'm taking my

time over this work, contemplating all aspects, trying to remember precisely how the fox looked the times that I've seen it. The whole morning passes. I'm pleased with the progress I've made, and though it's far from finished, this carving now looks somewhat like the animal it's intended to be.

Heading to the living room, I'm glad to notice, in the hall mirror, that the bruise and graze on my face, from falling off my bike, are nearly gone.

I press *play* on my stereo. Christmas tunes. I get the bag of presents I have for Pete, Camille and Owen, which I've already wrapped, and I find the cardboard box I've been keeping for packing them in. Along with these gifts, into the box I place a tin of biscuits, a decoration for their tree that I bought for them at that Christmas market, and some pink and white candy canes as I know Owen loves them. I know too that when they receive this package there will be great excitement for Owen: last year, Camille sent me a photo of him unpacking and putting the presents under the tree. It makes me prepare this box with care, as it's not just a parcel I'm preparing but the event of them receiving it. I realise I'm much more excited about all this Christmas stuff than I possibly should be, I am every year, but I don't care. I stand from the sofa, go to my stereo and turn it up a bit, as 'Mary's Boy Child' has just started. As the beat kicks in, I dance a few steps as I make my way back over to the parcel. I sing along, badly I'm sure, as I wrap the parcel with sticky tape and write the address.

I get ready to go into town. On my way out of the door, clutching the box under my arm, I grab the pile of cards I have to send, too.

In the queue, I've counted seventeen people in front of me. If it weren't for the fact that it's tight for this delivery to get to Canada in time for Christmas, I might just try another day. I check my watch though, and see I've actually got plenty of time to get back to the estate and open up the community centre. It's quiz night. I want to arrive early and get the heating on.

Finally at the counter, I complete a customs form for the gifts. I ask for thirty first-class stamps, for my cards. I pay, and the parcel for Pete, Camille and Owen is taken from me to begin its long journey across the Atlantic. Away from the queue, which has got even longer, I place a stamp onto each of the envelopes before dropping the cards into the post-box.

As I step into the street, I find that it's dusk already. The Christmas lights in town are bright and hopeful. I begin walking back to the estate when I feel the first cold needles of rain. Seeing there's a bus at the stop, the final passengers boarding, I make a run for it.

On the top deck I pick a seat about halfway back, as the bus shudders and pulls away. There are only a few others up here. A young couple are sitting at the front. He has his arm around her and they're giggling about something. I look away, see that the rain, heavier now, is streaming down the window and making the world watery. The couple there have made me think of that Christmas card, the unwritten one that I longed to write: *To Amber, Merry Christmas, from Daniel, Flat 157*. I really like her, which is silly I guess, as I only know her from a distance. There are her looks, I can't deny that, but there's also something

more important which I've noticed in the brief moments we've spoken. It was as though, when she looked at me, we connected, and when she spoke her words sounded very real. There's just something about her... I'm trying but I can't even pinpoint what it is; I'd love so much to discover it. I've got a crush on her, I admit. Been a long while since I had one of those. I've been single a few years now. Not even a date. I don't know why.

    I sigh.

    I know exactly why.

Stacey

It happened when I was twenty-nine. Old enough that I thought I knew everything, about myself at least. Then my entire world tilted. All it took, in this planet of billions, was one particular person coming into my life.

We met on a dating website. They were the new thing at the time. I'd met quite a few women for drinks or dinner during the year I created my profile. Though some dates were awkward, slightly tiresome even if we had a little in common, others were good, interesting or fun. Sometimes, I'd not get home until the following morning. But I had a feeling I wasn't going to meet *the one* in this way, that if it were ever to happen it'd be by chance. Like Mum and Ricardo in the popcorn queue.

Besides, the idea of meeting someone long term wasn't consuming me, as there was so much else going on. Pete and Camille had got married on a sunny day in June. Spencer and Joanne married that autumn. I was best man, twice. The wedding days were magical, captured in perfect photographs that I sit and take my time looking through sometimes.

Daisy-May was born. I'll never forget Spencer's call from the hospital, his words fast with excitement, the tears in his eyes evident in his voice. Then came Owen, the first new member of our family since Pete. This change felt barely believable until I saw his little, chubby face for the first time. His eyes were closed. I placed my finger in his palm and watched in wonder as he grasped it with his tiny

fingers.

When life, or, rather, everyone else's lives were busy with all these great things, one weekend I got into an online chat with Stacey. We liked some of the same music and books and I thought that if we met we might at least have a nice evening together. So I asked her out. We decided on a pub for the following Thursday.

In the back of my mind I looked forward to meeting her, though the week passed in a typical way. On the Thursday I took some time getting ready and chose my clothes thoughtfully, but I didn't have any big expectations as I travelled to the pub. Stacey had texted to say she was already there, had got us a table upstairs in the corner. When I reached the top of the stairs I recognised her right away from her profile photo on the dating site. She spotted me too, smiled and waved. As I sat opposite her, an odd feeling came over me: I knew that this date was going to be very different.

What surprised me the most, while we enjoyed drinks and bowls of chips, was how easy it was to talk to her and how good it felt to listen to her. She told of her life, her family, her work. She spoke of her dreams and I told her of mine. I thought perhaps we looked at life in the same way, and I'd never felt that with anyone before. As the noisy pub whirled around us, it was as if Stacey and I were on our own little planet, as though we'd known one another not for hours, but for years. The bell rang for last orders, and it was then, after we'd pulled our coats on at the end of drinking-up time, that we were kissing. I don't even know who reached out first.

I saw Stacey into a taxi, then began to walk home. The

night was clear, but my head wasn't. I'd had so much of the evening to take in that I needed that walk. When I got back to the flat I wondered whether I should text to say what a good night I'd had – unlike all the other dates I'd been on, I was very conscious of doing the right thing – but instead I texted Spencer. He called, even though it was late. I told him of all the things I knew about Stacey, of how something had felt very right when we were together.

'She could be the one, mate,' he said.

Given how relaxed he is about everything else in life, Spencer is curiously serious when it comes to relationships, which I'd only discovered when he met Joanne. As I relayed the evening to him, I remembered that the last thing Stacey had said was that she'd message me the following day.

'Definitely don't message then,' Spencer said.

So I didn't.

Half the night, I lay awake.

At work, after my greasy hangover breakfast and mugs of tea, I didn't feel as bad as I could have done from the lack of sleep. My mind was on things far more important than whether I felt rough or not. I'd never checked my phone so much. Just before lunchtime, when it felt that I'd waited for years, my phone vibrated and I grabbed it out of my pocket. The text was from Stacey.

We met that night for a meal, a couple of days later for a movie and soon after that I cooked dinner for us one evening at my place. As days turned into weeks, we went everywhere together, did everything together. We developed a routine of what we'd watch on TV, some of the programmes her choice and others mine. We enjoyed

walks in parks. We'd go to the pub, or for lunch in the café in town that I'd been to countless times in my life, but that was the thing with Stacey, she made the ordinary very, very different. The estate became a brighter place, even though it was still made of concrete. I would say I'd lived a good life even up to then, though time with Stacey made me realise there was another level of happiness. I'd never laughed so much.

We'd started calling each other girlfriend and boyfriend. I knew that nothing was ever going to be the same again.

15th December

My landline is ringing.

'Hello?'

'Dan the Man!'

'Hey, Pete!' A call from my little brother always cheers me up. I know that Camille and Owen will be there too, waiting to speak to me like every time. 'How's it going?' I ask, as I lay back on the sofa.

'All good here, been busy. How about you?'

'Not long been in from work,' I say. 'Just had dinner. Nothing much going on, to be honest.'

'Christmas soon, though.'

'I guess.'

'You don't sound like the usual big kid you are at this time of year?'

'I don't get excited about Christmas,' I say, teasing him.

'The one who makes everyone wear a Christmas jumper, who spends hours putting his decorations up?'

'Maybe.'

'The instigator of charades and other very annoying things.'

I laugh. 'You love it!' I say. 'But it's gonna be a quiet one this year.'

'Oh, yeah, Mum's going away with Ricardo soon, isn't she?'

'The big holiday.'

'You didn't want to go with them?'

'It'd be a bit of three's-a-crowd, don't you think?'

Pete chuckles. 'You might be right.'

'Plus, too expensive.'

'So, you going to Spencer's?'

'They'll be at Joanne's parents. I'm with them Boxing Day, though.'

'You gonna be on your own for Christmas, Dan?'

I cringe a little. 'Don't tell Mum, whatever you do.'

'She'll cancel her holiday if she knows you're on your own for Christmas.'

'Exactly! So you're not gonna mention it, right?'

Pete sighs. 'Right.'

I'm relieved. I know he keeps his word no matter what.

'Why don't you book a trip over here to visit us, then?'

'You think I got money for last-minute flights to Canada?'

'Ha! True. But you know we'd love you to be here.'

'Thanks. Maybe next year, eh?'

'Oh hang on, your nephew is tugging at my sleeve. He can't wait any longer.'

'All right, put him on.'

'Speak to you soon, bro.'

'Take care, Pete.'

I hear rustling down the line as the phone is passed, and feel a pang of longing to be there with them. The centre of attention is always Owen. He brings magic to a room. For him, nothing more important exists than laughing, playing, pretending to be naughty (while rarely actually being naughty), eating sweets, and dancing – music isn't even necessary for this. To look at, the boy is a mini version of Pete. His middle name is Daniel.

'Uncle Dan?'

'Hey, Owen!' I always feel a sudden sense of energy talking to him. 'How you doing?'

'I'm doing good,' he says. Whereas his dad has developed only a hint of an accent, little Owen sounds sort of Canadian already.

'Looking forward to Christmas?'

'I can't wait! Are you coming to see us?' he asks.

'Not just yet, but when I do it's gonna be great.'

'Yay!' he yells.

'Have you been good?'

'Yeah.'

'So you're expecting Father Christmas to bring you some presents?'

'Expecting lots of presents, been very good this year.'

I hear Pete laugh in the background.

Camille says something that I can't make out.

'Mommy wants to talk to you,' Owen says.

'OK, I'll speak to you another day soon.'

'Miss you, Uncle Dan.'

Now I *really* want to be there. 'Miss you too, buddy.'

The phone is passed again.

'Daniel.'

'Hi, Camille.'

'How's my favourite brother-in-law?'

'You mean your only brother-in-law?'

'That's the one.'

I smile. 'Not bad, thanks.'

'So you're going to be free for us to call you on Christmas morning?' she asks.

'Absolutely.'

'You know Owen's going to want to speak to you first

thing. No doubt he'll be up at 5am, as usual.'

This makes me happy. 'I can't wait. Though I'm glad I'm five hours ahead.'

She laughs. Then, an unusual brief moment of silence between us.

'Is there something you'd like to talk about?' Her tone suggests that there is.

'Not much going on here,' I say, slightly doubting myself somehow. 'Just work and stuff, y'know.'

She hesitates, conveying that she knows there's something I'm not telling.

My mind goes to Amber.

'OK then,' she says. 'We'll speak to you on Christmas Day.'

'I'll look forward to it.'

Owen starts yelling in the background: *'Bye, Uncle Dan! Bye! Bye! Bye, Uncle Dan!'*

I sit up on the sofa. It couldn't have been anything to do with my feelings for Amber that Camille sensed – perhaps it was just this uneasiness, which I've been having so much lately, that she picked up on. And all this being on my own for Christmas. Though I am of course happy for Mum and Ricardo and their holiday, just like I'm happy for Pete, Camille and Owen and the brilliant Christmas they're going to have too, I do feel somewhat dejected about having nothing to look forward to this year.

I stand and go to the window. Someone in the opposite tower, a floor or two above my level, has put lights on their balcony today, wrapped them around and around the railings. Resting my forehead on the glass, I peer down. Far below, in the garden of one of the terraced houses

alongside the green, inflatables have appeared: Father Christmas, a snowman and two reindeer. Then I notice, there on the green, something moving. In the light of a streetlamp, I see the fox. I watch as it sniffs at the ground for a while, then it's gone. I close the curtains, and head to the box room.

Settling at my workbench, I add fur detail to the back, chest and neck of the fox, taking my time, working as precisely as I can. As tiny wood shavings fall to the bench, it feels as though a just-emerging life is in my hands. It's this enjoyment of creation, the escapism of it, that has kept me doing this craft in all the years since Mr Silver taught me. The whole evening passes.

When I call it a night, I place the fox on the bench. I'm pleased with how it's turning out. It's mainly the face that still needs work, and its bushy tail. I stand, and as I'm about to leave the room to get ready for bed I stop and look to the fox again, sitting there, coming to life. I consider it, really look at it, try to figure it out, to figure everything out. Then, I switch off the light.

The Message

Stacey and I spent nearly all our free time together. As she shared a flat and I had my own, she'd stay at my place every weekend and some week nights, too. We still held hands as we walked through streets on days out, as we wandered shops or sat in cafes, cuddled as we lay on the sofa in the evenings and watched TV. Valentine's Day passed, my birthday then hers. We met each other's friends on nights out. I met Stacey's mum, too, and she met Mum and Ricardo, Pete, Camille and baby Owen, and of course Mr Silver. We went on a day trip to the coast with Spencer, Joanne and Daisy-May. Our lives had integrated. I'd had no idea just how perfect meeting someone, something so ordinary, could be. Everything felt very right.

It was probably for that reason that, when one day she said she was meeting a friend for a drink, I didn't think anything of it. I texted her back to say I hoped she had a good night, to look after herself and make sure she got a taxi home if it was late. I didn't ask who the friend was and at the time I didn't notice that she hadn't said. I spent the first part of the evening at the gym with Spencer, then watched a movie at home. When I went to bed that night I slept soundly, unaware that it would be the last time I'd do so for a long while.

It was full daylight when I woke. I picked up my phone, saw the time and was surprised there was no message from Stacey. Texting to ask if she'd had a good evening, really I was checking that she was all right.

I made breakfast, and as I began to eat I decided that if

I'd not heard from her in half an hour, I'd call. I thought then about what we could do later that day. It was a Saturday. She might be tired after her night out, and if so I'd suggest I make us dinner and we have a quiet night in.

My phone vibrated on the kitchen table. I grabbed it, was relieved when I saw Stacey's name. As I opened the message, saw the length of it, my breath caught. I knew.

Daniel, I feel awful for this, but I think it's best that I'm honest with you as you don't deserve to be messed around. Last night I met up with my ex-boyfriend. We hadn't seen each other for ages and he was in town for work and asked me if I'd like to catch up. To cut a long story short, we have a lot of history together and we've decided to give things another go. I realise this is going to be a big shock for you, as it is for me too. All I can do now is thank you for everything. It has been amazing spending time with you, and you truly are one in a million. I'm so sorry Daniel x

My chest felt tight. I became suddenly aware of how very unimportant and ridiculous I was, sat there at my little kitchen table fifteen storeys in the air with my eggs and toast half-eaten in front of me, my cutlery resting on the side of the plate I'd bought from the charity shop. I didn't know what to reply, or whether to reply at all, or if to ask for her reasons and see if I could fix them all. I was about to call her when a truly awful thought entered my head: what if she was with him, had been all night?

And who was this bloody ex, anyway? She'd mentioned one in passing before, like I'm sure I'd mentioned one or two, but I hadn't picked up the slightest hint that there was anything unfinished for her. I didn't know how long they'd been in a relationship for, or when they'd split up or why. I didn't even know his name, or what he looked like or

whether he had a good job and a big house, a posh car instead of a bike. To know these things suddenly felt vital. My mind a mess, I went to the kitchen window and looked out at the estate: concrete and windows, everything and nothing seemed the same. An elderly man in the opposite tower stood at his balcony and looked over the green below. I wondered if life ever made any sense.

I met Spencer for a jog that evening. I'd usually tell him and Pete everything, but somehow I didn't want him to know what had happened. I felt embarrassed. I decided I wouldn't say anything about it, but as soon as we met, the first thing he said was, 'What's wrong?'

We sat on a wall. I opened Stacey's message and passed him my phone, waited in silence as he read it. He passed my phone back to me, was annoyed, called Stacey a name and then apologised to me for it. Once he'd settled down, he gave me ideas for what I could message back, as I had none. Yet he didn't encourage me to try to save anything, said that it'd be hard to repair. I found this difficult to hear as Spencer is usually a fixer of things, not one to abandon.

'She's not the right one for you,' he said, with certainty.

We didn't jog that evening, we just sat there on the edge of the estate and talked, as the sun slipped away and the air became too cool for our shorts and T-shirts.

When I got home, I realised it was over in the way she hadn't texted me again, even though I hadn't replied all day. I was no longer a concern of hers. Her message hadn't even suggested a reply was needed, or wanted. I wondered whether that was the reason Spencer had told me not to try to save the relationship: to save my dignity. I had no idea what the nameless, faceless ex had that I didn't, but

whatever it was, it had been enough to end everything.

In bed that night I tried to find sleep, but of course I couldn't. My mind was flooded with unspoken questions. Eventually, I took my phone from the bedside table, opened Stacey's message and read it once more. After pressing the reply button I typed four words: *What can I say*. I hit send.

I stared at my message until the phone screen went dark and the room, like my heart, was drained of light.

17th December

I cycle to Spencer and Joanne's place, wishing I'd dressed more warmly. Everything is covered in frost: pathways, lawns, the naked branches of trees.

Arriving at their house, I'm pleased to see the ice has been scraped from Spencer's car windows. I push my bike through the gate into the back garden, where I'll collect it from later, then I go to the shed where he's hidden the key for me before they went out for the day.

He doesn't use his car much – they mostly use Joanne's. Budget and lack of need has kept me from ever buying one, though I do enjoy these odd occasions where I slip into a driver's seat and feel like a slightly different me. I turn the ignition, then switch the heating on before I pull out of the driveway.

Parking in one of the bays on the edge of the estate, I go to Mum's house. Letting myself in the front door, I see two large suitcases in the hallway. I've no doubt that Mum has packed them carefully and checked them at least twice. I notice she's put the decorations up, amongst them on the hall ceiling is a spray of mistletoe in the same place that she pins some of this plant every Christmas. She comes rushing down the stairs, a bag in each hand.

'Hello, darling,' she says, her excitement at the coming holiday clear.

'All right, Mum.'

She places the bags beside the suitcases.

'Dan!' Ricardo says, appearing from the living room.

'Thank you for offering to drive us.'

'No problem,' I say. 'Thought it'd be nice to see you both off.'

'We're stopping over in Hong Kong,' Mum says, as if suddenly remembering this fact that she's certainly impressed with.

Hearing her speak of far-off places makes me smile. A trip like this would've been unthinkable for Mum when Pete and I were growing up. Months back, while they were planning this holiday, she asked so many times whether I minded her being away for Christmas, whether I'd be OK, as though she felt guilty about the whole thing. I really had to make the point that it was all right, that I'm a big boy at thirty-four and I'd be going to Spencer's place anyway. This took some persuading, so I was relieved when they did finally book it. She and Ricardo have been saving so long for this holiday.

'Come into the kitchen,' Mum says.

As I follow, I'm surprised to see that she has decorations up there too, and through the living room door I see a tree. 'What have you decorated for, when you're going away?'

'I thought it'd be nice for you, for when you pop in while we're gone.'

'Oh, Mum. Thanks, but you didn't have to do that!'

I notice there's a load of food and drinks on the kitchen table. At a glance I see a net of walnuts, a Christmas pudding and a stollen loaf. A packet of beers. Crisps and crackers and dates. 'And what do you need all this for?'

'It's for you, too,' she says. 'It was going to be a surprise for when you came to water the plants, but seeing

as you're here…'

'Amazing!' I really am pleased with all of this.

She opens the fridge and points inside. 'And there's a cheese selection in here.'

'You know I love a cheese selection, Mum.'

'I wanted to make sure you had enough to eat and drink. You can take some of it to Spencer's on Christmas Day too.'

'I'll come round and pick it all up tonight.'

'Your present from me and Ricardo is there, and the other one was in the parcel from Pete. Take those home with you as well, to put under your tree.'

'I will do, thanks very much, Mum.'

'Are you sure you're going to be all right while I'm gone?' There's real concern in her voice, as though this is the very first time she's thought of this potential problem.

I'm going to have to be convincing or else she still could cancel the holiday, even though they're about to start their journey and their passports are in Ricardo's hand. 'Absolutely,' I say. I produce a big smile.

We leave the house. I place the heavy suitcases into the boot and the smaller bags on the back seat with Ricardo. As we set off through the estate towards the main road, Mum turns in the passenger seat and looks back to the house, as though checking that the place hasn't gone up in flames or something already.

She faces forward again, and sighs. 'You'll pop round every day or two, then?'

'Of course.' Mum has given instructions over the past few weeks, though I know she's going to go through them again now, just to be sure I've got it.

'Plants will need watering once a week. Open and close the curtains, so it looks like there's someone home. Turn a few lights on and off.'

'Stop worrying, Mum.'

She sighs once more.

I put the car heating on again. It really feels like the first true winter's morning of the year, even though Mum's wearing a floral dress and a straw sun hat.

I park at the airport then walk into the terminal with them, ignoring Mum's pleas for me to just drop them off so I don't have to pay for parking. This place is so chaotic, people walking in all directions. Lifts and escalators. Announcements from speakers. Everyone looking about themselves a bit confusedly. Ricardo leads the way even though he doesn't know where he's going, pulling his large suitcase on wheels, looking for the check-in desk.

While we queue, Ricardo, who has planned their trip meticulously, tells of all the places they'll be visiting. Their *itinerary* he calls it, which sounds far too official and unlike a holiday for me, though I don't mention this as Mum's excited by it. Besides, it's probably best that they have a plan, to make the most of it, as who knows when they'll get a holiday like this again. It's their trip of a lifetime, perhaps. As I watch Mum, her arm resting on Ricardo's shoulder, I think about how great it is that she met him, even how cool it is that they've met at this later point in their lives. There's hope for us all, perhaps. I wonder if they might get married. I'll ask Mum about it when I've got her on her own sometime, but that's rare these days.

At the departures area, we're saying our goodbyes. I

have a sudden thought back to the day when we were here with Pete, Camille and Owen when they left, indefinitely, for Canada. There'd been a lump like a pear in my throat as Pete and I hugged and he whispered into my ear, *I won't be gone forever, I promise.* Mum and Ricardo are off for just over three weeks. Right now, I'm not sure why, three weeks feels very long.

'Have a brilliant time,' I say. 'And don't forget to send me postcards.'

Mum kisses my cheek. 'You take care. I hope you have a great Christmas at Spencer's house.'

'Thanks, Mum, I will.' On Boxing Day.

'Make the most of the peace and quiet,' Ricardo says. 'We'll be back before you know it!'

I watch as they show the guard their boarding cards, then go into the security area. Before they turn a corner and go out of sight, as I knew she would, Mum looks around. She waves one last time. I wave back. As she smiles, turns and walks away, she puts her hand on her sun hat as though she's just felt a warm summer breeze that might sweep it away.

The Decision

After Stacey, evenings and weekends were long. My mobile rang less. My small flat felt enormous. I like to think I can adapt to change, but after we separated, life was different in a way that I couldn't quite get used to.

One afternoon at work, six months after our last contact, I got a text from Stacey. I hadn't deleted our messages from before, so this new one appeared just below the last I'd sent – *What can I say* – pointing out the incomplete place where we'd left things.

Daniel, I made a terrible mistake. It didn't work out with my ex, as I should have known and just as my friends had told me so. We split up again after a few weeks and I've been wanting to send this message ever since but didn't feel that it was fair of me to. I think of you all the time, of what could have been and of what I threw away. I made the worst decision of my life. I'll completely understand if you want nothing to do with me now, but I have to try at least, to ask if you can forgive me. I'd love to see you.

I had somehow known I'd hear from Stacey again. What we'd had together had been so significant that it couldn't possibly have been closed forever the way that it was. Spencer also thought that I'd hear from her again. However, the news that all this time she had actually not been in a relationship with her ex was a big surprise. All the heartache and the sleepless nights suddenly felt pointless.

It was Spencer who I first told of the message, when we met in the gym that night.

'I told you she'd be back!' he said, looking somewhat

triumphant. He even did a sort of fist pump. 'So, what you gonna do then? Ball's in your court now.'

I didn't like that. I didn't want any kind of control. That wasn't how Stacey and I were. 'Meet her, I guess.'

Spencer shook his head, though he was smiling. 'Maybe the two of you will sort it out after all,'

'Maybe.' I felt a burst of hope, thinking those amazing times really could be possible again.

'But don't reply too quickly,' Spencer advised.

I agreed. I really didn't have to rush to reply and perhaps I should make her wait a little, so that she didn't know I'd been hoping for this day. I was also sure that she'd see right through this, but I'd go through the process nonetheless. I decided I'd reply the following day.

But that night, I picked up my phone:

I'm surprised to hear from you. I guess we could meet.

I deleted that.

It's surprising but good to hear from you. We can meet if you want to talk.

I deleted that too.

I'm so pleased to hear from you Stace. When can we meet?

I left that draft there. I would hit *send* in the morning. I'd sleep on it.

But of course, there was no sleep that night. There was me, wide awake, the flat filled with moonlight and doubt. Did Stacey and I have anything to go back to? Were things with that ex really finished? Those months, not quite a year, that we'd spent together felt like a time capsule, might be something best preserved rather than watered down by trying again and failing. My memories of us were pristine.

I got out of bed sometime in the small hours and went

onto the balcony. The night was mild, the estate almost sleeping, just some teenagers sitting far below on the green, being too inconspicuous to be doing anything they ought to be. I looked across the estate, at the night sky. As I glanced from star to star, I had a strange thought that perhaps I wouldn't reply to Stacey in the morning.

The next day at work, I somehow carried on as usual. I didn't read her message again, and trying to ignore my phone altogether I put it on silent and left it in my pocket.

I called Spencer in the early evening, and he was surprised that I hadn't replied to Stacey.

'Well done,' he said. 'I didn't think you'd be able to hold out this long, mate.'

After our call, I made myself dinner. I watched some TV. I went to the box room and worked on a wood carving. While I did all these things, I was trying to convince myself that Stacey and I had something to go back to – I wanted very much to believe so – but I wondered whether I might always be fearful of losing her again. I'd likely be suspicious of who her friends were, of where she was, who she was out with or what she was doing. The dream of our relationship had been ruined really, with her and that ex, whose identity was still unknown to me. In my mind, he was just a blank face on a tall, muscular body. He was also long gone, it seemed from Stacey's text, but for me he was somehow still present.

That night, when I went to bed, I took my phone out. I read her message again, saw my drafted reply: *I'm so pleased to hear from you Stace. When can we meet?* Slowly, character by character, I deleted that message until there was nothing but an empty screen and a flashing cursor. I put my phone

on the bedside table, and that night, to my surprise, I slept more soundly than I had for the previous six months.

Days… a weekend. Two weekends passed. I had not replied to Stacey.

Weeks later, I was sitting in Spencer and Joanne's garden on a warm evening. We were at their patio table, having a beer, when the subject of her came up.

'You sure you're doing the right thing?' Spencer asked. He'd been adamant at the time of the break-up that the relationship was irreparable – he'd known more than anyone how hurt I'd been, even though I hadn't actually told him how much it had hurt – but he'd changed his mind since. He thought I should get back with her.

'I think so,' I said. 'It's all over.'

'I'm so sorry it didn't work out for you, Dan,' Joanne said. 'You deserve better.'

I took a swig from my bottle. 'I dunno about that, but thanks,' I said. Then I looked away, down the garden to where Daisy-May was playing, as my eyes were suddenly stinging a bit.

I heard them whisper briefly, though I didn't hear what was said.

Joanne got up. 'I'm going to get us some snacks,' she said.

Once she'd gone, Spencer stood. He took a bottle from the bucket of ice and water on the table, opened it, and as he set the bottle down in front of me he patted my shoulder. 'You'll be all right,' he said.

As soon as I got home that night, as I stood in the hallway, I took my phone from my pocket. I deleted all the messages Stacey and I had ever sent to one another. They

were gone in seconds. I took a deep breath, was sure that I'd made the right decision in not replying because I'd thought about it so thoroughly. It's unsettling to think how much I thought I was right about that.

19th December

I call the lift.

Stepping inside, I press *G* a few times. In the graffiti-covered, mirrored rear wall, I open my jacket and check how I look. I'm wearing a light blue shirt which I took my time ironing. Dark blue chinos with a wide black belt. These shoes I only wear once in a while and they look good as new.

Soon after the lift has begun to drop, it slows, then stops. I'm a bit irritated at the delay as I'm already running late. When I see Amber standing there, however, I don't mind at all.

'Hello.'

'Evening,' I say.

She enters the lift holding a carrier bag that clinks with glass bottles. She stands beside me, so that we're not facing one another but the doors, which are closing again. I realise that this is a moment: for what, I'm not entirely sure.

'How are you?'

She turns to me. 'Very well, thanks.' She has dangly silver snowflake earrings and the most beautiful brown eyes I've ever seen. 'Off to a friend's place, for a movie and a takeaway.'

'Sounds good.'

'And you?'

'Meeting some mates for a meal. It's our Christmas get-together.'

'How lovely,' she says.

The lift has annoyingly reached the ground floor.

Some teenage boys, wearing hoods and caps and tracksuits, one on roller boots, brush past us as we exit and they enter. They all look at Amber before they look to me.

'All right, Dan,' one of them says.

'All right,' I say.

'Looking very smart, Dan,' another says, placing his hand on my shoulder for a second as he passes.

'Thanks.'

'Have a good one, Dan,' another says, and others cheer at this. One whistles.

Pretending I've not heard, I push the main door and hold it open for Amber.

'You're popular,' she says, smiling as she goes through.

The estate is lit with streetlamps. Our breaths are white clouds. I'm a bit embarrassed. 'I know them from the community centre, that's all. Those boys come to football practice. I volunteer there.'

'I didn't know there was a community centre.'

I'm pleased that she isn't rushing off. 'It's that building.' I point across the green.

'What goes on there, then?'

'We have sports practice for the youngsters, bingo nights, quiz nights, dart nights. A disco once in a while. All sorts of stuff, as long as it's cheap, as we mostly run on donations. Like, on Christmas Eve, we're having a fundraiser. There'll be mulled wine and carols.' I want to say that she should come to this, but I think I might be talking too much.

'That sounds lovely,' she says.

There's a moment of silence.

'Got cold now, hasn't it?' I say.

'It has! It'll be frosty in the morning.'

'Yeah, I think so.'

Another silence, and in just a couple of seconds it goes from fine to awfully uncomfortable.

'Which way are you going from here?' she asks.

I point towards town. 'I'm meeting them in the Queen's Head. You?'

She nods the opposite direction. 'The bus stop.'

'Ah, right.'

'Have a good evening,' she says.

'Thanks. Enjoy your movie.'

She turns to walk away. 'Was nice chatting to you.'

'And you,' I say, and I walk away, too. *It was really, really nice chatting to you.* I'm relieved I managed to get through the conversation without making myself look stupid, I think. Though I'd love to glance back, I don't.

As I pass alongside the ditch, I think of the last time, the only other time, I really felt something for a woman and of how badly that turned out. But this is somehow different. Amber, who I don't even know, has got me feeling all out of sorts in a way I can't quite understand. Just as I'm thinking this, the fox crosses my path. It stops, looks in my direction, then carries on its way on silent paws.

I've been to the Queen's Head many times before. The old building is a series of rooms where it used to be a house, long ago. The doorways are so low that I have to dip my head to pass through them. There are black beams in the brick walls. Big smoke-stained open fireplaces. The place

aches with age yet bustles with life. I find Spencer and Joanne at the bar.

'Hey!' Joanne says. She hugs me. 'Haven't seen you for weeks!'

It sometimes unsettles me how quickly time passes between seeing a friend, acquaintance or family member, and how there are only so many of those times in a lifetime. 'Good to see you,' I say.

'Dan.' Spencer, smiling, shakes my hand, while placing his other hand on my upper arm as though he's checking my gym progress, which he might well be doing. 'I'll get you a pint.'

With our drinks, the three of us move into the restaurant area, to the table we've booked. Soon, others arrive: Spencer and Joanne's neighbour, Joanne's mum and sister, Spencer's brother Anthony, the parents of Daisy-May's best friend. I've met them all before. At the centre of this jumble of people, seated one each side of our round table, are Spencer and Joanne. They make an effort every Christmas to organise a gathering.

Chatter flows all around us and across our big table, as a basket of bread is passed. Soon, our starters arrive. The mood is good. The food is delicious. Familiar festive music is at just the right volume and the fireplace nearby us roars.

Seated to my left is Anthony, whom I've known since I was a teenager. Joanne's mum, Diane, is to my right. As Anthony appears to be chatting up Spencer's neighbour, I mostly speak to Diane. We work in similar jobs and talk about that, but by the time our mains are being cleared I know of her newly discovered love of yoga and she of my wood carvings, particularly the fox I'm working on.

Now the whole group are talking together. We're reminiscing Spencer and Joanne's wedding, teasing them about what a good match they are.

'And you, Daniel,' Spencer's neighbour says. 'Are you seeing anyone?'

'I'm not, no.'

'But he's got his eye on someone,' Spencer says, making me cringe.

'Who is she?' Joanne's sister asks.

'I don't know her, really. She lives in the same block as me, a few floors down.'

'What's her name?'

'Amber.'

'And are you getting to know Amber?'

All eyes are on me. 'We've only spoken a couple of times. There was the post thing,' I say to Spencer, but then I realise that no one else at the table knows what this means. 'The postman put a letter for her through my door by mistake, so I took it down to her.'

'That was convenient,' Anthony says, smirking.

'A sign,' Diane says, and everyone agrees.

'I saw her in the lift tonight, actually,' I say, feeling somewhat happy to be speaking of her, but I know nothing will ever happen with Amber, that to her I'll only ever be that bloke who lives upstairs.

'Did you speak to her?' Spencer asks.

'Yeah.'

'What about?'

'I briefly told her about the community centre.'

'And?'

'Then I just said something about the weather.'

There's a murmur of giggling at the table.

'What?' I ask.

Spencer rolls his eyes, smiles. 'Could you actually be any more boring, Dan?'

I smile back. 'Shut up!' Everyone laughs, either at me or with me, and I don't really mind which.

The waitress has brought our desserts to the table.

Joanne holds her phone out to her. 'Would you mind taking a photo for us, please?'

'Not at all,' she says.

We shuffle our chairs and lean in. Hands on shoulders. Glasses raised. Anthony gives a thumbs-up.

The waitress is aiming the phone at us. 'Say *cheese*!' she says.

And we do.

And the moment is captured not only by the picture but also in my mind. I know that this is one of those evenings I'll remember fondly.

A Friend

I never did reply to that text from Stacey. She sent another message a couple of weeks after, again asking to meet, wanting to make up for what she'd done. I didn't reply to that one, either. When I was just about able to ignore the third message, the last, I really thought I was moving on.

It was nearly a year later that I regretted not replying. On my birthday, I was at a Wednesday matinee, the theatre in town nearly deserted. I'd celebrated the previous Saturday by going for a meal with Mum and Ricardo, Spencer and Joanne and a couple of people from the office. I'd also booked the day of my birthday off work, though of course no one else had, nor should have. I thought I'd try to do something memorable with the day and that's how I found myself there at the theatre that afternoon. I was enjoying it. When the interval began, I turned to my side and went to say something about the play, but there was just an empty seat beside me; I realised that was where Stacey should be. The realisation that she and I were finished forever was unexpected and horrible, a cold draught of an unseen ghost sweeping through the stalls. I left the theatre.

When I reached the flat, I cried. I'd not done so since I was young; that time when I'd realised Dad wasn't coming back. I couldn't shake off the thought that I'd missed the chance, when Stacey had sent those messages, to restart our unfinished story. Worse still, I'd stubbornly believed that passing it by had been the right thing to do. Yet I

could have tried to accept her reasons for going back to that guy, even if I couldn't, didn't want to, understand them. Though I tried not to, I cried more, realising the upset had been building for months, that I'd been blocking it out.

I took the stairs to the ground floor, because the flat was suffocating. The distress was worryingly unfamiliar, like my body was not my own, as I was OK all the time usually. That day though, I wasn't. I needed something – an anchor, a friend.

I knocked on Mr Silver's front door.

It took a while for him to answer, as always with his advancing years. When he opened, he looked at me curiously. I wondered if my eyes were still red, whether I looked as bad as I felt, though he didn't say anything about it. I followed him towards his living room, watched him, to see how he was. One hand on his walking stick and the other on the wall as he passed along the hallway. He was having one of his more difficult days, but his sparse grey hair was neat and his shirt clean and pressed as always.

I saw him to his armchair.

'I'll make us tea,' I said.

'Lovely. Thank you, Daniel.'

He'd refused help for so many years, but more often now he accepted these little things being done for him. I wished he'd let me do more, help him with his house or take him for a day out once in a while, but he always declined, saying he didn't want to be any trouble, leaving me reluctant to push the point, not knowing if he really wanted to go out at all.

While the kettle boiled I checked his food cupboards,

then the fridge as I took the milk out, and it felt good to be doing something, to not be thinking about Stacey, to be thinking about someone else. I was pleased to see he had a good stock of food – I'd often bring him in a few bits. His great-nephew, Luke, who was only just an adult and who I'd never crossed paths with, had started staying over once in a while and brought supplies with him too, even though he lived a long way away. I squeezed our teabags, stirred.

I settled into my usual armchair. Our mugs of tea steaming on the table between us, a moment of silence ensued in the living room I'd visited since I was a boy. A room where nothing much changed: the furniture, wallpaper, paintings and ornaments, the wood carving of a pineapple that I'd gifted him years before. There was even the same old clock on the mantel above his gas fire, and though it didn't chime any more, it still worked. For a few minutes there was just the stillness of the room, that clock ticking, me and Mr Silver. I considered telling him what was troubling me, though decided not to. He'd known Stacey and I had separated quite a while before. I would have felt embarrassed to tell him that I was still upset over it, that I'd only just realised the loneliness in that there had been life, and now there was life after Stacey.

'It'll get easier with time, I promise you.'

I looked up at him. At first I wasn't sure what he was talking about, but as we held eye contact, I understood that he knew not only that there was something upsetting me, but exactly what that something was. And he'd spoken so clearly, with such certainty, that I knew what he'd said was true.

Lots of days at work, occasional celebrations, boring weekends and good weekends, a difficult time once in a while. It was like I, along with the people in my life, somehow settled into our lives and got on with them. I was in my thirties by then and I'd got to know myself a little more, instead of always having the future and a different version of myself planned. And days passed, weeks, months. Years, too. I was still on my own, but it was OK. I'd see Spencer and Joanne's happiness, even though they'd rowed a bit, and Pete and Camille's too, even though they were stressed sometimes that they were always short of money.

Then there was Stacey, or rather, there *wasn't* Stacey. When she came to mind, which she often did, it was usually with feelings of regret. It's strange how even though we only lived seven miles apart, we never crossed paths in a supermarket, or on a bus or a train. We had no mutual friends and never made any after. I never cycled past her on the street or saw her in a pub. It was quite some time before I stopped looking out for her – just a glimpse would have been something – though I don't know whether it would've made me feel good or bad. I even had casual conversation topics ready, for the occasion we bumped into one another, but the meeting never occurred and eventually I forgot my prepared conversations. It was another couple of years before I felt settled, without everything having some kind of comparison to what I'd felt during my time with Stacey, but Mr Silver had been right. Things got easier. In the end I was happy being on my own, was no longer looking for a partner at all.

Life carried on. Pete and Camille moved to Canada, to

the town she grew up in and where she'd got a job offer so good that it couldn't be refused. Owen and Daisy-May grew from babies into children. Mum and Ricardo were out enjoying life, and if I popped to the house unannounced I might find it empty. I got a promotion, a pay rise. I refurbished my flat. And of course, I still regularly visited Mr Silver. He was doing well, even though he'd slowed down considerably. He'd gone from old to some other level of elderly, and I could see the difference in his movements, his skin, his eyes. I'd go for tea, or for lunch, or to borrow a tool from his workshop, but the main reason I went was for our chats. We would talk forever, Mr Silver and I.

One day, when I was in his living room, on the shelf I saw a small carving of a tree. Something he'd completed recently and I guessed hadn't found a home for yet. I noticed it was less refined, didn't have the exquisite finish of his usual work, and that worried me. I'll always remember that carving, as it was the last that Mr Silver ever completed.

21st December

It's bake sale day. Nearly everyone has made an effort, though they'd be pushed to get out of it, what with all the posters I'd put up and the reminder email I sent yesterday. People have made cakes, pastries, pizzas, all putting my attempt at baking to shame. Tim the office junior decided to spare us his cooking and instead bought doughnuts from the shop, as did Nathaniel from Marketing, who arrived with supermarket sausage rolls. Colleagues have gathered and are chatting beside the table I've set up outside the kitchen. I'm pleased to hear coins dropping into the donations pot. Though most already know what the collection is for, I gladly tell them about the community centre, of the difference it makes, especially for the young and the elderly. They are perhaps more generous as they know I volunteer there. I even see Norman from Customer Services is approaching, and he's notoriously tight.

'Which ones did you bake, Daniel?'

I know he's expecting me to have bought something from the shop. 'Those ones,' I say, pointing. The plate is still full, the only one that has yet to make a sale.

'Oh,' Norman says.

Though he's one of my favourites at work, I love proving him wrong.

He glances over the other selections on the table, at the brownies and the flapjacks, then to Marie's black forest gateau that looks to die for and is two-thirds gone already.

'I suppose I'd better take one of your biscuits then,

seeing as I asked.'

I'm stunned to see him drop a five-pound note into the pot. 'Take a few, Norman, treat yourself. It's Christmas,' I say, picking three and placing them onto a plate for him. I don't tell him they're not biscuits at all, but fairy cakes that didn't rise in the oven and just burnt a bit.

At home, I go from room to room, switching on lights and heating. I tip the collection pot onto my kitchen table and count one hundred and six pounds thirty. This isn't bad, I think, and though I can't remember exactly what last year's total was, I'm sure it was under a hundred. I add a twenty from my wallet, put it all into a money bag and into a drawer. Along with whatever we get at the fundraiser on Christmas Eve, I'll pay it into the community centre's bank account when everything reopens after the holidays.

I begin to cook, and as I do so a gloomy feeling comes over me as I remember there's nothing happening this Christmas, that I'll be here on my own. It makes no sense to feel this way, when everything outside is so cheerful – bright lights and decorations are everywhere. But still, I've got this feeling. I think I think too much.

My phone pings. I take it out of my pocket and see it's a message from Camille, telling me that their parcel has arrived, that they look forward to opening it on the 25th. I feel better again.

After I've eaten, I wash my plate, dry it, put it into the cupboard. I make a hot chocolate and go to the living room. As I'm about to close the curtains I notice another few flats in the opposite tower have put lights on their balcony. I slide the doors open to take a look. The lights

are multicoloured, flashing, abundant. It's chilly out here tonight, though strangely not as bitter as it was earlier. I glance around the estate, down at the green, up at the sky. It's full of clouds. I heard on the radio that there might be snow on the way. They say that every year though, a possibility, they say, but it never happens. The only white Christmas I can remember is when Pete and I were boys. It snowed heavily one night and it was a week before it thawed. Along with the other kids on the estate we built snowmen, snowwomen, whole snow families down there on the green. I've always had some romantic idea of walking with a girlfriend in the snow, our arms linked. This has never happened.

I go to the box room and work on my carving. I focus on the texture of its fur, and though I'm concentrating, my mind is elsewhere. I'm thinking about Christmas again. Loads of people are on their own for Christmas every year. For me, this might be the only time. It'll really be fine, now I think about it. I live on my own anyway. I enjoy keeping my own time and making my own meals. I like watching whatever I want on TV and to have the peace to read a book instead, or have a sleep on the sofa, or a long bath, or all of those things in one night. And I have all the food and drinks from Mum, and the cheese selection that I'm having to resist eating already. I can go out for a jog on Christmas Day, enjoy the empty streets, and how many people can do that? Everything is going to be cool. Maybe. Going to Spencer's on Boxing Day, that's something I have to look forward to. Besides, next year I might spend Christmas with Pete, Camille, and most importantly of all, Owen.

My evening is wonderfully lost in carving, until it's late,

far too late for a work night. After I've shaped the almost unseen line of its mouth, I realise that there is nothing else for me to do; the fox might be complete. I pick it up, examine it all over, before placing it back on the bench. We watch one another for a moment. I'm satisfied, think it might be the best work I've ever done. I've carved its face with the precise detail I intended, though showing through that is something I've created by accident: it has some kind of look about it. The fox regards me as though it knows something that I don't.

Amber

It was late summer, earlier this year. The evening was warm and bright. I was cycling home from work and as I neared the tower I saw a lad crouching beside his bike. Even with his back to me, I recognised Tommy. I'd seen him grow up from the little boy who'd hold his mum's hand everywhere they went, to a teenager who's as tall as me and always wears the hood on his tracksuit pulled up. He's a good kid. As I braked and stepped off my bike, he looked up.

'All right, Dan,' he muttered.

Beside him was a puncture repair kit, the tiny tube of glue, sandpaper and patches, spilled on the ground. 'You all right there, Tommy?'

'Got a flat, I think.'

I stood my bike and crouched beside him. I squeezed his back tyre. 'Looks like it. You got your kit there, then.'

'Mum got it for me ages ago. Never used one before.'

'You want a hand?'

Looking as though he didn't want to admit that he did, he nodded.

I slipped my backpack off. 'Let's get that wheel detached then. We'll get the inner tube out and take a look.' I always have a few things in my bag for these occasions: a pump, tyre levers, a repair kit of my own, as I've been caught out too many times before.

I showed him how to remove the tyre. 'If we pump it up again, we might be able to find where the puncture is.'

Tommy took the lead with this, feeling the inner tube,

tilting his head to listen for the sound of escaping air. He found the problem spot, then in the tyre the thorn that'd caused it.

'With this little bit of sandpaper, rub around where the puncture is.' I demonstrated, before letting him continue.

'What do we need to do this for?'

'It will help the patch to stick,' I said. 'Looks good, Tommy. I think that'll do.' I picked up the little tube of glue. 'You just need about this much, and spread it around like this.'

He watched closely.

'Now we'll leave that for a minute.' I heard a vehicle behind us. I glanced around and saw a removal van parking in a nearby bay. I turned back to the wheel. 'Do you wanna open up one of those patches?'

'Sure.'

'You'll need to peel the back off. That's it,' I said, once he'd got his fingernail under the edge of it. 'I'll hold the inner tube, you put the patch on and press it down firmly.'

As he did this, I heard voices. I looked around and saw a woman talking to two removal men as they opened the rear doors of their van. Then, she walked towards us, or rather, towards the entrance of the tower. She glanced down at me, sitting on the ground, inner tube in my hands. I looked away, but once she'd passed us by I turned to her again, couldn't take my eyes off her, a set of keys dangling from her fingers. She held the doors for the men with their boxes, then she was gone and the door was slowly closing.

I realised Tommy was smirking at me. Embarrassed, I returned my attention to the tyre.

'Eleventh floor,' Tommy said.

'Huh?'

'She'll be moving into eleventh, flat seven – saw the family from there moving out yesterday.'

'Oh, right,' I said, as if this was barely of importance. I didn't look up to see if he was smirking again, though I expect he was. 'Let's get this tyre back on,' I said.

We both stood as we replaced the tyre, then attached the wheel.

'Keep an eye on it. If you notice it going down again, give me a shout.'

'You're a star, Dan,' he said, shaking my hand as though we'd just struck a business deal. He swung his leg over the saddle, then rode around me a few times, testing it all out. 'Thanks!' he called, as he set off on the path to the green.

I pushed my bike into the tower. As I waited for the lift, I wondered if that woman might be on her way back down. I ran my hand through my hair, straightened out my T-shirt, but when the doors opened the lift was empty.

Later that evening, I went jogging with Spencer. He came to meet me and we took our usual route around the green, along the ditch to the main road, to town where it was quiet by then with the shops closed, then back to the estate. We did this route twice, as the heat of the summer's day faded and the sun set, leaving the sky orange. When we were back at the tower, we sat on the wall outside for a breather.

'I saw this woman moving in earlier. Eleventh floor, apparently.'

'Did you do your neighbourly bit and introduce

yourself?'

'Nah, she was with some removal guys. Plus, I was helping one of the lads from the block fix his puncture. But she was…'

'What?'

I sighed. 'I dunno,' I said, to the golden sky. 'Do you ever just, like, get a feeling?'

When Spencer didn't answer, I turned to him.

He looked amused. 'You like her or something?'

I shrugged. I was going to say that I'd hardly seen her properly, to dismiss it all, but I had seen her properly and I hadn't felt quite right since. 'Do you ever just get a feeling, that like, something really, really good, or bad even, is about to happen?'

Spencer shook his head. 'I don't, to be honest.'

At the distant sound of laughter, I turned and saw that far away, on the pathway on the opposite side of the green, was Mr Silver, moving very slowly on his walking frame. Beside him was a much younger man, younger than me, who I didn't recognise. Strangely, he had Mr Silver's bag in his hand. 'See you later, mate,' I said to Spencer, distractedly, as I set off across the grass towards them.

23rd December

I wake, roll over and hit my alarm. Under the duvet I'm warm, but my hand, which must have been outside as I slept, is cold. Reluctantly, I get out of bed, stretch and yawn as I go to the kitchen. I fill the kettle, drop slices of brown bread into the toaster. I'm tired, but as I wake further I begin to feel positive about the day ahead, as not only is it Friday but also the last day at the office before Christmas. This kind of thing always makes people more friendly and chatty. I expect hardly any work will be done. We've got lunch booked at a pub near the office and we'll all head home after that.

I make coffee, spread peanut butter onto my toast and go to the living room where I place the plate and cup onto the table. I pull the curtains open… and gasp. The balcony is covered in snow. When I slide the doors I hear shouting and laughter. I shiver as the bitter air creeps over me – I'm wearing only my pyjama bottoms and T-shirt. Stepping out, snow crunching beneath my slippers, I peer over. Way down there, the green is a blanket of white. Some kids are building snowmen, others throw snowballs. A child pulls another on a sledge with rope attached to it, one of them taller, both fully covered in their coats and hats and gloves as though they're made of fabric. I think of me and Pete, of that one time we had snow like this and had played out there. Mum had wrapped us up, just like those two.

I go back inside and close the door. I pull a hoodie on and turn the heating up. As I eat breakfast, I look to the

opposite tower where the balconies are snowy, just like mine, where others stand at their windows to take in this magical winter's morning, just like me. I wonder if it might still be here in two days' time, a white Christmas, though I guess it'll have melted or been rained away by then. No snow falls now.

After showering and dressing for work, I place the gift I have for Marie into my rucksack. I won't be able to cycle in today's weather, so I prepare to walk: boots, my longest puffer jacket, scarf. I tug my woollen hat down over my ears.

Leaving the tower, each step squeaks in fresh snow that's a few inches deep, the footprints of others lead in all directions. I take careful strides, am making progress through the estate, when I notice paw prints, too. I suspect they belong to the fox. I wonder where that beautiful creature might be now and of what it makes of this snow, which must be the first it's ever seen. It takes a while to walk to work, though with this altered wintry world and my thoughts to occupy me, I'm in no hurry.

I arrive at the office and take my boots off at the door. 'Morning,' I say, as I pass the receptionist, but she's tapping away on her keyboard and hasn't noticed my arrival, or has perhaps ignored it. Over recent days, we've asked her a few times to join us for lunch today, but she's got a stock of excuses not to spend any more time with us than she has to.

Boots in hand and only grey socks on my feet, I walk to my desk. I've a pair of shoes beneath it and I slip them on. I'm alone in the office. From the sound of distant conversations and laughter it seems that everyone's in the

kitchen. I switch my computer on, then head to join them.

'Hey Dan!' Marie says. She's wearing a hairband with antlers on it.

'Morning,' a few others say.

'Morning all.' I feel as though I've just reached the pub on one of those nights where everyone has had a few already and are more pleased to see me than they should be, though this isn't the pub and of course this lot aren't tipsy. They're just drunk on snow. It's shifted the mood of everything. Even a couple of strangers wished me a good morning on my way here.

'We're having breakfast,' Marie says, a mischievous curl at the corner of her lips. She holds a plate towards me which is piled with homemade mince pies. The room is filled with a warming pastry scent, even though the office is cold. I take a pie gratefully. My healthy eating is truly gone until the new year now and I really am fine with this.

We arranged this meal back in summer, when Christmas was so far away that it seemed silly to plan for it, but with lessons learned on how early everywhere gets booked up and with time passing at the speed that it does, we reserved our place. Now, crackers pulled and paper crowns on our heads, we wait keenly for our traditional roast to be served. All around us are tables of other office folks doing the exact same.

Our food arrives and it's worth the wait. The sprouts burst in my mouth, the Yorkshires melt as I chew them, the parsnips are wonderfully sweet. We all agree that the roast potatoes, which are cooked to perfection, are the highlight, though they're beaten when pudding is served.

Steaming before I drench it with cream, the first mouthful is magic. The unique taste of this fruity pudding embraces me with the warm cloak of Christmastime.

Finishing my glass of white, then leaning back in my chair with my hands on my stomach, I feel as though I'd love to eat the whole meal all over again, but I couldn't fit in another thing.

We are back in the office and packing up for the day, or rather, for the year. In my bag are a few leftover pies, which Marie has wrapped in napkins. I take the cards from my desk, then my advent calendar with its one remaining closed door. I pack my gifts from Marie: a tin of biscuits, a box of chocolates. She gives me a hug and a peck on the cheek.

'Have a lovely time,' she says.

'And you. Have fun,' I say. 'And you too, Norman.'

'Enjoy your Christmas, Dan.' He shakes my hand. 'All the best.'

It's as though we're all about to embark on separate, slightly uncertain journeys, until we reunite on the other side.

With them gone, I finish packing my stuff. There are only a few others remaining here, Tim the office junior and Nathaniel from Marketing amongst them. Across the open-plan office we exchange best wishes, then I pass through Reception as I'm zipping up my jacket.

'Merry Christmas!'

I stop suddenly. I turn and find that the receptionist is looking at me. She's almost smiling. I think she just spoke to me. 'Merry Christmas to you too,' I say.

She *is* smiling! Then, she looks back to her screen.

It's nearly dark as I walk home, but everywhere is still bright with snow even though none has fallen all day. Although it's difficult to walk in now – icy in some places, slushy in others – the snow has brought a calmness with it. There are fewer cars on the road, less noise. A feeling of tranquillity, which doesn't live around here, is visiting us.

It's lovely to be leaving work behind for the holidays, though it feels different this year since most of my Christmas fun has already happened. Whereas all the others from the office are going back to their families, to housemates or friends, I'm not. There's still the community centre fundraiser tomorrow, but after that, all there is to do is relax. Recharge the batteries, as they say. It'll be a different Christmas this year, not how I would have wanted it to be at all, but it might still be all right.

I've stopped off in the supermarket. I'd usually be rushing to football practice on a Friday, but as most of the crowd had festive plans we decided to miss tonight, and I can take my time having a browse here. I choose sprouts, potatoes, carrots and parsnips and put them into my basket. A box of stuffing. Gravy granules. I go to the fridge and look at the turkeys. It'd be a bit of a waste, I think, to buy one, to cook one, just for me. In fact, perhaps all this veg in my basket, along with that jar of cranberry sauce, is a waste. Is there really any point in me buying all of this when it's just me this year? I sigh, decide to go to the counter with it all.

Reaching home, I slide my key into the lock, flick the light switch, close the door behind me. The flat seems dreadfully quiet, the evening ahead very long.

In my box room, I sit at the workbench and look at the fox carving. Working on this has been such a part of my routine over recent weeks that I'd forgotten I'd completed it until I sat here. I pick it up, look at it closely. Of all the carvings I've done over the years this is my favourite, and the thought takes me back to the day I was a boy in Mr Silver's garden workshop, when I completed the owl. I wish Mr Silver was sitting on a stool beside me here at the workbench so that we could look at this carving together, discuss it, share the moment, but there's just me and the fox, looking at one another.

I go to the kitchen and get a big bag of crisps from the cupboard, open them and stuff some into my mouth. As I'm crunching, I start to make myself a hot chocolate. Not a great combo, definitely not the healthiest, but it is Christmas after all. Well, nearly.

I take my crisps and drink to the living room and switch the tele on, where I hope I'll find a decent festive movie to watch, but before I settle on the sofa I go out onto the balcony to see how the snow is doing. There's still a covering, except on the pathways where it's partly been trodden away. I look at the Christmas lights everywhere, at the night-time estate. Just as I'm about to go back inside I notice the fox, way down there in the pool of light from a streetlamp on the edge of the green. It's sitting, a bit like it is in my carving. Then I realise it's sitting *exactly* in the position it is in my carving, other than it's looking upwards. It watches me a moment, then trots away, vanishes amongst the darkness of the overgrowth beside the ditch.

CHRISTMAS EVE

A lady is working out. A bored-looking personal trainer leans against a chest press, his arms folded, watching the TV, which is tuned to a music channel. A cleaner polishes the mirrors with a yellow cloth, even though they're already sparkling. Then there's me. The gym is only open until lunchtime today. It looks like most aren't rushing to fit in a last-minute workout before Christmas, and I don't blame them.

Finishing up, I take my jacket, scarf and boots from my locker and realise I'm the only one in the changing rooms. It's usually packed in here, a challenge to find space on a bench, the air filled with steamy shower mist and loud chatter. It feels eerie now, as though everyone has scarpered after hearing some big news that I've missed.

It hasn't snowed again. The pavements are slush and ice. Walking home, I notice people out and about. I see two guys, could be brothers, wearing tinsel around their heads, then a woman with a Christmas jumper. Many are travelling, it seems, heading in the direction of the station or waiting at bus stops. They carry bags as though they're off on holiday, but I expect this lot are going home to their family and friends. Others are doing last-minute gift shopping and buying final supplies of food. There's a familiar sense of anticipation in the chilly air today, a feeling that something's about to happen. I smile at the thought. Owen will be speaking of little other than the arrival of Father Christmas.

As I continue through town I see a nativity scene I'd not noticed on my recent visits, perhaps it was hidden by crowds of shoppers. I stop and take a look. It even has real hay. Mary and Joseph, the baby Jesus in a manger, Three Wise Men bearing gifts; I feel a moment of peace, before I go on my way.

Entering the estate, I look up at the two towers. Though both have the same eighteen storeys of identical windows and balconies, in the one on the left I know exactly which flat, which windows, are mine. Home. I can't complain, really. I'm living a very fortunate life up there and I never forget that, even though the flat is often cold and the lift breaks down regularly. And my day alone tomorrow will be just fine. Besides, I've not got time to dwell. There's loads to organise at the community centre for the festive fundraiser tonight. I'm meant to be opening up at four, for preparations, but I need to go home and get ready first. I glance at my watch, try to quicken my pace in this messy snow.

I'm in good spirits as I shower, brush my teeth, splash some aftershave. I decide which jeans I'll wear, pair them with a Christmas jumper. I dig around in the back of a drawer in my bedroom, find the thick socks I'm looking for. I slip my fingerless gloves on, then my scarf and hat. I check myself in the mirror in the hallway. Not my best look, but at least I might not freeze – it's dark outside already, will be very cold. I get the lift to the ground floor, zipping up my jacket on the way.

I leave the building. 'Look at that,' I say, to no one. It's snowing again. Not like yesterday, this is another level of

snowfall, like a blizzard, fierce and beautiful, looks as though it should be roaring but all is silent. It's already covering yesterday's slushy leftovers, making everything smooth and fresh. I cross the green.

Unlocking the door of the community centre, I flick the light switches then turn the heating on full, as it doesn't feel any warmer in here than it does outside. The old decorations, which I'd put up a few weeks ago, are looking a little sad, have definitely seen better days. We must find new ones next year.

It's not long before fellow volunteers arrive. A few are unpacking the mince pies they've baked to be sold tonight. A couple are preparing mulled wine in the little kitchen. Others are organising the prizes for the raffle. The carol singers are having a warm-up in the sports hall. I really hope there's a good turnout after everyone's made the effort here, and that people are in a generous mood with their donations.

The plan was that we were to have all of the events inside the hall, but after I hold a quick group discussion, and possibly a moment of madness from us all, we decide to move the tables outside, to beneath the shelter by the bike racks, to appreciate the wintry scene. The wind has eased now, and the heavy snow falls gracefully. We couldn't have dreamt that we'd have this setting for our special night. When we turn the festive music on, up loud so it can be heard outside, it feels like the event has truly begun.

People begin to trickle from the two towers, emerge from the pathways and alleyways that lead to the green. More follow, and soon the place is busy with people

greeting their neighbours and friends with hugs and handshakes, a kiss on a cheek or two, some exchanging cards and wrapped gifts. Children throw snowballs, chase one another across the green, which is lit with streetlamps and snow. Soon, it seems as though the whole estate is here and more from the nearby neighbourhoods. The festive fundraiser in full swing.

I'm working with Fiona on one of the stalls. We're going between here and the kitchen, carrying mince pies and warm cups of wine out into the cold, as people throw coins, sometimes a note, into our donations bucket. I'm seeing so many familiar faces, some I've known my whole life nearly – I even had a catch-up with Pete's old mate, Terry, here with his wife and kids, and I'd not seen him for ages. I'm meeting a few new people, too. We've turned the Christmas music off and the crowd's conversations are quiet now, so that the carol singers can be heard from their spot on the edge of the green. And still, snow continues to fall on our estate.

'Have a break, Dan,' Fiona says. 'You've been here longer than all of us.' She hands me a pie, a steaming mug. 'Go!' she says. 'Take ten minutes.'

There's a lull at our stall now, anyway. Most people are over by the carol singers. I wouldn't mind a break, actually. 'Thanks, I will do.'

I wander from the stall and place my mug on a snow-dusted table. I bite into the pie. Listening to 'The Holly and the Ivy' being beautifully sung, watching the snowball wars, it really does feel like Christmas. Good to see everyone enjoying their night, and me... I don't think I'd want to be

anywhere else right now.

My phone vibrates in my pocket.

'You all right, Spence?' I say quietly, though from where I stand I'm a safe distance not to interrupt the carols.

'Where are you, Dan?'

'At the Christmas festive fundraiser, remember?'

'Oh no, I forgot! I'll bung you a tenner when I see you on Boxing Day.'

'Let's make it twenty.'

'Fine.'

'Thanks. I was going to—'

'Dan, unless it's, like, mega-important, shut up and listen please. I've called for a reason.'

That's got my attention. 'All right.'

'Are you sitting down, Dan?'

'No.'

'You're gonna flippin' need to, mate. You know the photo, from the other night?'

'What photo?'

'At the Queen's Head. Joanne asked the waitress to take it, remember?'

'What about it?'

'Jo posted it online. You know what she's like, puts pictures of everything on there.'

'I'm hardly ever online, mate.'

'But anyway, you've been spotted.'

'Spotted?'

'By Amber!'

It takes a moment for this to register. 'Amber from downstairs?'

'It turns out she works at Jo's company!'

The coincidence takes the air from me for a second, my voice a whisper. 'You're kidding me.'

'She sent a message to Jo a little while ago to wish her a Merry Christmas, said she'd seen the picture and recognised you, started asking about you. Then, two minutes later, they're on the phone.'

'Oh, God.'

'She was saying that she lives in the same block as you. Then she started asking all this stuff… what you're like, whether you're single. Dan, whether you're *single*!'

I don't know what to say.

'Jo told her we've been mates for years, then started gushing over what a nice bloke you are. I've actually got doubts now that my wife likes you more than me!'

I laugh a bit, but really, my mind is elsewhere.

'Anyway, Amber has sworn Jo to secrecy that she asked, and Jo has sworn me to secrecy too, and now I'm swearing you to secrecy or Jo will kill me.'

I laugh again.

'Oh, no, she's coming. Gotta go,' Spencer says, then ends the call.

I put the last piece of pie into my mouth and chew everything over: the photo, Amber's call to Joanne, Spencer's call to me. I blow onto my wine before I take a sip, its spicy scent bursting through like open arms. Warmth soaks through my fingerless gloves, but the air is so chilly that there is something clear and new about it, makes every breath feel like a blank sheet of paper. Spencer must have got it all wrong, surely?

I'm still trying to make sense of what he's told me when

the carollers begin 'Silent Night'. It's by far my favourite carol. I look to them, over there at the edge of the green where they stand in a huddle, holding lanterns. I watch and listen, lost in the beauty of it all, in this estate on Christmas Eve, where snow is falling and singing carries through the night. I feel so alive that there's a lump in my throat, because I know that in this moment something truly magical is happening: life.

'Hello, Daniel.'

I turn to the voice. Amber is approaching me. I'm frozen, and it's nothing to do with the snow and ice. 'Hi,' I say.

She's wearing a bulky coat and a knitted scarf. Her hair is hidden beneath her blue hat. 'We meet again,' she says.

I nod, unsure of what to say.

She looks towards where the kids are throwing snowballs and chasing one another. She sips her drink; she must have just got it from Fiona. 'Good to have the snow, isn't it?' She turns back to me.

'It's great.'

'Nice for the kids.'

'True,' I say. 'Though to be honest, I was pretty excited myself when I opened the curtains yesterday morning. I couldn't wait to get out in it.'

I didn't mean it to sound funny, but it's made her giggle. 'Same,' she says.

For a moment, neither of us say anything, but there's nothing awkward or silent here. There's just me and Amber, laughter and kids calling, and of course the carol singers.

'How long have you lived around here?'

'All my life,' I say. 'I used to live in one of the terraces over there, with my parents and little brother, before I bought the flat in the tower.'

'So this is truly your home.'

'Yeah.' I already know when she moved in, though I'd better ask. 'How about you?'

'Just arrived this summer.'

'Oh, lovely.' I think back to that very first time I saw her, as I helped Tommy with his puncture.

'All ready for Christmas?'

I sigh. 'Not much going on this year. My brother and his family live in Canada now, and my mum's on holiday.'

'You're spending it with friends?'

'Just Boxing Day. You?'

'Sounds like there's two of us on our own this Christmas,' she says.

'You're not with family either?'

'I had to work up until yesterday, then I'm in again before New Year, so didn't think it was worth attempting the journey, what with most of the trains not running next week. They live in London.'

'That's fair enough.' I take some of my drink. It's cooled already. Snow still falls all around us, the air is full of it.

'It's funny,' she says. 'The other day, I couldn't decide whether I should buy myself a proper Christmas dinner, y'know, turkey, sprouts, Yorkshires, stuffing, cranberry sauce and all that, or whether to not bother with it all this year.'

'That *is* funny,' I say. 'I did the exact same thing!'

'I just bought a few microwave meals in the end.'

'I got the whole lot,' I say. 'Except the turkey. Thought it'd be a waste, just for me.'

'I guess you're right,' she says. As if remembering something, she glances at her watch. 'My goodness. I've got to dash. I'm late for meeting one of the girls.'

'All right,' I say, a pang of disappointment in my chest.

Amber finishes her drink. 'I'll just drop this mug back,' she says.

'I'll take that for you.'

'Oh, thanks.' She passes it to me. 'Sorry I have to rush off.'

'It's OK,' I say casually, as though I'm not gutted at all. 'Was lovely to chat.'

'Yeah, it was.' I have a sudden, unwelcomed thought that this could be, probably will be, all there is to the me and Amber story, the beginning and the end, even after Spencer's call.

'Well,' she says. 'Goodbye, Daniel.'

'Bye, Amber,' I say, as she turns to leave. It feels good to say her name. 'Merry Christmas.'

She turns back. 'Daniel?'

'Yeah?'

Snowflakes are gently settling on her coat, on her hat. 'I don't suppose...' she says.

I swallow.

'I don't suppose you fancy meeting for dinner tomorrow?'

I can't say anything back.

'I could heat the ready meals,' she says. 'You could bring your vegetables, and it would be great to chat more and—'

'I'd love to,' I say, barely able to believe this moment has come.

'Lovely!' she says. 'Around twelve?'

'Sounds good.'

'I live in number—'

'I know.'

She smiles. 'I'm afraid I don't have any decorations up.'

'I've got decorations.'

'Is that you inviting me to your flat instead?'

I suddenly remember, I didn't bother to put the decorations up in the end, for the first time ever, because I was on my own. But I can fix this. 'Sure. It's flat 157.'

'See you tomorrow, Daniel.'

'See you then.'

She steps away through the snow. I watch her as though she's a miracle.

With the big event finished, heading home with my bag heavy from the night's fundraising, my mind is on my food cupboards and what's inside them. I'm wondering whether I have enough food and drink for tomorrow, so when I reach the flat it's the kitchen I go to first. I'm pleased to find that with the stuff I'd bought and the good stock from Mum, there's plenty of everything.

My flat is tidy, but somehow not tidy enough. I clean the kitchen, the fridge, replace tea towels and hand towels with fresh ones. I scrub the toilet, the sink, the chrome taps until they shine. I put a new loo roll out even though there's over half of one left. I mop the floors, get the vacuum cleaner out, dust the lampshades and the photos in frames and the wooden mallard on the shelf.

I take the boxes of decorations from the cupboard. Shaking the snow globe with Father Christmas inside, I watch as the flakes fly around. The weather in there looks like outside here tonight. I place the globe on the coffee table. Standing on a chair, I hang snowflake mobiles, foil garlands and paper bells, my thumb numb from pushing drawing pins into the ceiling. On my front door I hang the wreath I'd forgotten I had.

Reaching into the box again I find a nest of green wire: the tree lights. As I begin to untangle them I look to the corner of the living room, between the TV and the balcony doors where I always put my… 'Oh, no,' I say. 'I didn't buy a tree.' The first year since I moved in that I haven't bought one, which is a real shame what with Amber coming tomorrow. Then, I remember: Mum's got one.

Back in the lift, I'm zipping my jacket and taking my hat from my pocket. It's still snowing heavily as I cross the green. All is blanketed. Every doorstep, window ledge and gatepost is covered smoothly in white.

I reach the house and step inside. Switching the light on in the hall, I look up at the decorations Mum has hung from the ceiling, along with the spray of mistletoe. It feels as though the house was waiting for me. Taking my boots off on the doormat, I sprinkle the surrounding carpet with snowflakes and ice and somehow a bit of mud. As I go into the living room I breathe in the scent of pine and feel grateful. Mum, who'd only bought this tree and decorated the house for me when I pop in and out. If only she knew how she's saved me right now. I quickly strip the tree of its baubles, tinsel and lights. Finding some brown string in a kitchen drawer, I tie it around and around the branches.

I'm heading back across the green, carrying the tree on my shoulder, following my footprints that are already half-hidden. There's no one out now, not even the fox. A rare moment, here: in the middle of the estate, snowflakes blowing all about me, I somehow feel as though I'm the only person in the world. Then, as I approach the tower, from one of the lower flats I see a little boy and girl peering from a lifted curtain. They don't notice me – they're too busy watching the sky, wishing, waiting, hoping.

The tree is redecorated and looking pretty good, if I say so myself, though I've made a mess of the living room. When I've finished vacuuming again, it's just gone 11:30. Time for bed. I'm about to switch the light off when on top of the cabinet I notice the present that Mum left for me, along with the one Pete had sent. As I place them under the tree, I realise that I've forgotten possibly the most important thing of all. A gift! I don't have anything to give to Amber. It'd be weird for me to hand her something expensive or big, but just something small, a token… I'm disappointed that I have nothing. Then, through the open living room door, across the hallway, through the open door of the box room, the wooden fox looks back at me from where it sits on my workbench. I sigh with relief. The world is definitely on my side tonight.

I get into bed. Even with my mind full of the events of today and the unknown things to come tomorrow, I feel that I'm going to sleep well.

I pick up my mobile to text Spencer.

Amber is coming to my place for dinner tomorrow.

Because it's late and he's away, I don't expect he'll see

my message until morning.

Seconds later, my phone bleeps.

ARE

YOU

KIDDING

ME?

He's sent his message not only in capitals but as four separate texts.

The phone bleeps again.

How?

I text back.

It just sort of happened.

I'm about to text him again when I glance at the clock. Nearly twelve. *I'll catch up with you properly tomorrow!*

Putting my phone on silent, I place it on the bedside table and switch off the lamp.

I'm beginning to feel tired, but my mind is warm with anticipation for Christmas Day. I wonder where Mum is, what it looks like there, how with the time difference she might be having Christmas morning already in a hot sunny day. I think of Pete, Camille and Owen, and with their time difference they'll still be in the early evening of Christmas Eve. And here I am, fifteen floors above the earth and my heart in the clouds.

I feel sleepy. For some reason I remember that night, when we were just boys, in our small shared bedroom with the bunk beds, when Pete had played 'Mistletoe and Wine'. *I'm giving Father Christmas a sign,* he'd said, *that we're here.* He'd been hoping that the magic of Christmas was going to help us get the things we dreamed of.

Just as sleep is taking me away, I think that, distantly,

perhaps from the green, I hear the tinkle of sleigh bells.

CHRISTMAS DAY

I open an eye. It takes me a moment to realise that the noise is my landline ringing, that this is what's woken me. I stumble out of bed and down the hall.

'Hello?' Barely awake, my words are just a croak.

'Merry Christmas!' Mum and Ricardo shout together, startling me into the day.

'Merry Christmas,' I say. I sit on the sofa and rub my tired eyes as a happy feeling soars through me: it's Christmas Day! 'How's it going down there?'

I'm waking up now, as I listen to Mum, then Ricardo, speak about their tour of Australia, of the places they have visited and the people they've met. Their enthusiasm tells that they're having the time of their lives.

'It's boiling here,' Mum says.

'We've got snow,' I say.

'You've never!'

'There's a thick covering.'

'How lovely, for Christmas, too,' she says, though I don't think she's wishing she was back here. I can picture her at the other end of the line, wearing that straw hat, and sunglasses, in her hand a glass of bubbly that I've a feeling isn't her first of the day.

We finish our call. I've only put the phone down a few seconds before it rings again. I know who this is going to be. I pick up the handset, am about to say hello, when I hear a little voice; and it makes my whole day even though it's barely begun.

'Uncle Dan! I'm wearing my new jacket!'

I've been trying to keep busy all morning. For some reason, I have a feeling that Amber isn't going to show up. I don't know why I think this, as nothing from our conversation last night suggested it, but I've just a feeling. I'm trying not to check the time too much.

I shave and shower, iron a shirt, decide against the shirt and take it off. In my wardrobe I find a festive jumper; not one of my silly ones but just something red and knitted, and smart. I wear my chinos that look like new even though they're not. I take my time combing my hair. Splashing some aftershave, I wonder if I might be making too much of an effort, before trying to wipe some of the scent away with a wet flannel.

I carry the little kitchen table into the living room and position it near the balcony doors, so we can enjoy the wintry view when we eat. After draping it with a tablecloth, I set the cutlery and the salt and pepper grinders. I open all the windows to give the flat a quick airing, then close them again and turn the heating up.

I'm back in the kitchen. I've washed and peeled the veggies so they're ready for the oven, now I'm tipping a bag of nuts into a bowl, crisps into another. Thinking about opening a beer, I think again.

My mobile is ringing. Spencer. I knew he'd be calling, to catch up on the gossip.

'All right, Spence?'

'Dan! What's going on with Amber then? Merry Christmas, by the way.'

I laugh. 'Merry Christmas.'

'Spill the beans.'

'Well, she came to the festive fundraiser last night, we got chatting, and yeah, we ended up arranging dinner for today.'

'Amazing!'

'Well, if she turns up and that.'

'Why d'you think she's not gonna show up?'

'I dunno,' I say.

'Bit of nerves creeping in, eh?'

'Anyway, even if she does, I mean, what's the chances of us actually hitting it off? At best, it might be dinner with a nice bit of conversation.'

'Or you might both live happily ever after?'

'Funny. I appreciate your positivity, but I doubt…'

'You still there, Dan?'

'There's… there's a knock at the door.' I glance at the clock. It's just gone twelve.

'Good luck, Dan!'

'It might just be one of the neighbours with a tin of biscuits or something, or sometimes the boys from football practice pop round with a Christmas gift?'

'Stop messing about and go and let her in!'

I sigh. 'OK, speak to you later, Spence.'

Taking a deep breath, I walk down the hall.

Amber's hair is parted into plaits, each tied off with green tinsel. She wears a Christmas jumper that's far more ridiculous and brilliant than mine. She has a carrier bag in one hand and a bottle in the other. She beams. 'Merry Christmas, Daniel!'

This is happening. 'Merry Christmas!' I say.

She leans forwards, puts her hand on my shoulder and,

surprising me, goes to kiss my cheek, and though we just sort of bump faces, two kiss sounds fill the hall.

'Come on in,' I say. Once the door is closed she passes the bottle to me. It's fridge cold. I look at its label, as if I know all about wine or something. 'Lovely. Let's get this open then, shall we?'

'Sounds good.'

In the kitchen I take two glasses from the cupboard. 'Can't believe it's still snowing.'

'I don't think it stopped all night,' she says, looking from my kitchen window and seeming as happy about it as I am.

I pass her glass.

'Cheers,' we say.

After we've taken a sip, she puts hers on the side and picks up the carrier bag she'd brought with her. She takes out two ready meals.

'Are you more of a lasagne man, or a spinach-and-ricotta cannelloni man?'

I look at the pictures on the packaging. 'I'm both, as it goes.' Something makes me wish they were both the same. 'Which one would you like?'

'Asked you first!' she says.

They both look nice. 'We could do fifty-fifty?'

She seems impressed with this.

You know how it feels sometimes, when things just happen by themselves and go just the way you'd hoped they would? Well, that's how Christmas dinner with Amber is going.

She likes the tree and the way I'd placed the table

beside the balcony doors so that we could watch the snow. Our microwave meals with festive veg, stuffing balls, Yorkshires and cranberry sauce, and the pudding and cream we've just polished off, have gone down perfectly. We have some background tunes on and the flat is toasty-warm.

We have not stopped talking for the past couple of hours and I know a good few things about Amber now. I know her tastes in music, movies and books, the kind of things she likes to do at weekends. Where she hangs out with her friends and what kinds of pubs and restaurants she prefers, though like me she doesn't go on nights out much at all. She sees the future positively and wants to train to become a teacher. Her nephew is called Oliver and he's a similar age to Owen. She doesn't like sprouts (I ate hers) and she loves parsnips (she ate mine). She's good at telling jokes. And I know that I like her. A lot.

We're still at the dinner table. Amber is glancing around my living room.

'I've just realised how many Christmas cards you've got. You must have a lot of friends.'

'They're mostly just from people on the estate.'

'And you've got presents under your tree too, still to open.'

I turn to the tree, lean down and pick up the first parcel. I read the tag aloud, even though I know what it says. 'To Dan, love from Mum and Ricardo.' I place the present on my side of the table, before reading the tag on the next one. 'To Dan, love from Pete, Camille and Owen.' Then I pick up the third parcel. 'Oh,' I say. 'Looks like this one's for you.'

'For me?' she asks, looking pleased.

I pass the gift to her. Last night I'd found a box for the fox, wrapped it and put a red ribbon on it. 'It's nothing exciting, I'm afraid.'

She turns the package over in her hands as though she's trying to guess what it is. Then she rips the paper away, opens the box and looks intrigued as she places the fox onto the table. 'Wow,' she says. 'That's caught me by surprise.'

'Good!'

'It's fantastic. Look at all that detail,' she says, running a fingertip over the fox's head as though she's stroking it. Then, she looks to me. 'Well, you didn't have time to go shopping for this since we only made plans last night, so that means either you can predict the future, this gift was intended for someone else, or you've picked this off of your shelf or something and wrapped it for me. I see you've another carving over there,' she says, motioning to the wooden mallard.

'It's the first one,' I say, trying to be smart. 'I can predict the future.'

It wasn't funny really, but Amber laughs anyway. 'I love it,' she says. 'Thank you so much.'

'You're welcome.'

'I feel bad now that I didn't bring you anything.'

'Your company is present enough.'

'Good answer,' she says, winking. 'Now, open yours.'

I tear the wrapping from the package that Pete and Camille had sent and find that it's a jumper, not very unlike the one I sent for Pete. The gift from Mum and Ricardo is a dressing gown and slippers. 'Well,' I say, 'that's made me

look like an exciting kind of guy, hasn't it?'

Amber giggles. 'We all need a dressing gown and a pair of slippers.'

'True,' I say, as I clear the paper away. Then I notice the time. 'I'm sorry to interrupt the afternoon, but there's someone I need to visit and drop a present off to.'

She seems a bit surprised, as though I've done something unexpected. 'I'll head home and let you go.'

'Sorry, that wasn't what I meant!' I definitely don't want our time together to end so soon. 'I could drop the present off really quickly then come back, but actually I'd love it if you'd come with me. Then we could have some more food back here after, maybe watch a movie or something?'

'Sounds good,' she says, seeming relaxed again. 'Who are we visiting?'

From the sideboard I pick up the bottle of sherry, wrapped in a twist of tissue paper, that I've been so looking forward to delivering. It brings a smile to my face as I say, 'An old friend.'

It's been a few weeks since I've seen Mr Silver. It's baffling just how quickly time passes. I used to visit every few days but I do so a little less since his great-nephew, Luke, moved in, perhaps because I have less reason to worry. I liked Luke since we first met back in the summer, coincidentally the evening of the day I saw Amber moving in.

We cross the green, pathways out of sight beneath the thick snow that our boots sink into. There are a few people out and about, kids playing and folks heading off to somewhere, just like we are. To save Amber having to go back to her flat, she's worn one of my coats and hats. She

has linked her arm in mine.

We approach Mr Silver's house. His holly wreath is dusted in snow. I knock on this door that I've knocked on so many times in my life and every Christmas Day for the last thirty-ish years.

'That's Mum's house there,' I say, motioning to next door as we wait.

'How lovely that you've not moved far from home,' Amber says. She looks to the little conifers that Mum has in pots on either side of the doorstep. They're sprinkled with snow, too.

Luke opens, wearing a red paper crown from a cracker. 'Dan!' he says. 'We were just wondering where you...' He notices that I'm not alone.

'Luke, this is Amber,' I say.

'Great to meet you,' he says. 'Come on in, it's freezing out there.'

After taking my boots off I go into the living room. Mr Silver, also crowned, and looking well, is in his armchair. I'm pleased to see he's wearing the cardigan I got him recently. 'Hello, Mr S,' I say.

'Daniel!' His eyes light up.

I lean down to greet him. Every time we see one another it feels great, significant, like a reunion somehow, even though I see him often. 'You doing OK?'

'Oh yes.'

'There you go,' I say, as I hand him his gift.

'Very kind,' he says. 'Yours is under the tree.' He notices Amber now, coming into the room with Luke. 'And who have we got here, then?' he asks, with the same interested, half-knowing expression that Luke had just

worn at the front door.

'Amber,' I say.

'Who?' he asks, putting his fingertips on the back of his ear and turning it towards me.

'Her name is Amber,' I say, louder. We need to speak up a little for him these days. 'She lives a few floors down from me.'

She steps forwards to shake Mr Silver's hand. 'We've just had Christmas dinner together,' she says, having already picked up that she needs to raise her voice.

'Well, isn't that lovely,' he says.

Amber nods.

I don't sit in my usual chair, which is unofficially Luke's now, and instead I settle on the sofa. Amber is beside me.

'We've just had ours, too,' Mr Silver says, looking to the table and the bowls with only the smallest remains of pudding and cream.

'Can I get us all a drink?' Luke asks.

'Yes please,' both Amber and I say, as Mr Silver passes his nearly empty glass to Luke, for topping up.

Mr Silver and Amber have hit it off. She's talking to him about the estate and how this is her first Christmas since moving to the area. He's telling her of his decades living here, how I used to live next door and of how Mum still does but she's on holiday in Australia. Amber accepts the news as new.

'Have you heard from your mother?' he asks me.

'First thing this morning,' I say. 'They're having a great time.'

He looks genuinely happy at hearing this.

The two of them continue to chat and I leave them to

it. I look to the TV, a new one. A festive film is playing. The volume is muted, but I've seen the movie so many times before that I know exactly what's being said. Beside the TV is a tree, covered in baubles and in tinsel, in chocolates wrapped in foil. As I glance around the room, I notice some changes. It appears that Mr Silver's house is no longer rooted in the past. There are still the same old carpets, but their colours are vibrant, as though they've had a professional clean. Everything seems a bit brighter and I can smell air freshener. Such things I would've been happy to have kept on top of for him all these years, though he always liked to look after himself.

Luke, however, after finding a job in the area, has got stuck into things over the months since he moved in, perhaps with less awkwardness as he's family. There are some recent framed photos of relatives mixed in amongst the old paintings. The house's identity is still Mr Silver through and through, but there are signs of new life. The latest addition, it seems, is this big flat-screen TV, which Mr Silver points out to Amber proudly, as though it's the only one in the world.

'Had that telly in my bedroom at Mum's house,' Luke says, coming through the living room door with a tray full of glasses. 'Thought we might as well get it mounted here.'

'I watch a film nearly every night,' Mr Silver says mischievously. 'After he's gone to bed for work.'

'Lucky I've got earplugs.'

It warms me to see how they jokingly interact with one another. Mr Silver had been slowing down for years, but Luke has got him out more and isn't afraid of insisting that his great-uncle does stuff. He's got a wheelchair to help

with trips to the supermarket, coffee shops, to the library or the garden centre. They've even been to the cinema. I think Luke's energy, too, has made a difference; he's only twenty-odd, has enthusiasm for everything. Though Mr Silver has a lot of problems with his joints, I'd say his spirit seems a few years younger than it used to.

It strikes me that I could perhaps not have been feeling so dejected about the prospect of having Christmas alone, could surely have spent more of the day with Mr Silver and Luke instead of just this usual quick afternoon visit, if only I'd said. Then, on second thoughts, I rather like it that they've had their first Christmas dinner together, just the two of them. Just like me and Amber.

'Did you not fancy coming for the festivities at the community centre last night?' I ask.

'What's that you said?'

I lean a little closer, speak a little louder. 'There was a Christmas event at the community centre last night, did you not know about it?'

'Ah. We were there,' Mr Silver says. 'Only briefly, it was too cold for me. We saw you, rushing around you were. We didn't like to disturb.'

'You should have,' I say. 'I haven't seen you for weeks. I was going to knock when I posted your card through the door. There was a light on, but it was late.'

'Well,' he says. 'We're all here now. And I know you're busy with work and all sorts of things.'

'This whole month has flown by.'

'Oh,' he says. 'Your mother was round for a cuppa before she went away. Mentioned you're carving a fox?'

I glance at Amber, who looks to me in surprise. I turn

back to Mr Silver. 'I finished it,' I say, feeling embarrassed.

'What?'

'I finished it!'

'It's absolutely beautiful,' Amber says. She looks happy.

'Wonderful.' Mr Silver clasps his hands. 'You must bring it here one day, so I can see it.' He's said this to Amber, as though he already knows that the fox belongs to her now.

'We've got cake,' Luke says, as if suddenly remembering. 'A Yule log. Who's up for it?'

It turns out we all are.

He glances at his watch. 'I'll get it quickly now, before the Queen's Speech comes on.'

'I'll give you a hand,' Amber says, following him to the kitchen.

I look to Mr Silver, who's aiming the remote at the TV to change the channel for Her Majesty. I feel so at home in his company. It's always felt like this when I'm with Mr Silver, my friend who reminds me that life endures. I know nothing about the first half of his because he's never spoken of it, and I've always thought there might be some unfortunate reason for that; in the hall hangs a small, framed, black-and-white photo of Mr Silver as a young man, and beside him is a young woman. But at every juncture of my life he's been here, making the world make sense again with a few calm words. He is my constant. My teacher. I'd go as far to say he's my hero. He looks up, catches me watching him, beckons me over to sit in the armchair beside him.

'Well,' he says, 'Amber seems very nice, doesn't she?' He's trying to speak quietly, his lips exaggerating the words

as though he's conveying some scandalous gossip, which I've never heard him do.

'Yeah, she really does.'

'Looks like you get on well. A good match, I'd say.'

At hearing this I feel the great tension, which I'd barely acknowledged was present, release within me. When did that uneasiness begin? Has it just been there over these past weeks that I've found myself thinking about everything, about the past, where I am and where I'm going in life? Or did it start back in the summer perhaps, when I first saw Amber, unpacking the removal van and I thought, I knew… *something.*

He winks, raises his glass. 'Merry Christmas, Daniel.'

I pick up my wine. 'Merry Christmas, Mr Silver.'

It has almost stopped snowing, just a few flakes drifting in the air, as we leave Mr Silver and Luke to enjoy the rest of their day in front of the TV, eating and drinking, chatting and laughing as I'm sure they will be.

'Just need to pop into Mum's house, do you mind?'

'Not at all,' Amber says.

I slide my key into the lock. 'She's worried that people will know the place is empty. I've been given instructions that I'm to leave some lights on and to turn them off later, open and close curtains, stuff like that.'

'Then you'd better do as you're told,' she says, as we take our boots off again.

'She hasn't got much to worry about,' I say, as we go down the hall. 'There's not much trouble on the estate and a burglary would be a first.'

'I'm sorry to break this to you,' Amber says, as we

reach the living room door. 'But it looks like someone's already been in and stolen her Christmas tree.' She smirks as she points to the empty holder, to the heavy scattering of pine needles on the carpet where there's also a dropped bauble with its green plastic hook still attached. 'You know anything about this?'

'Ah,' I say, caught out. 'There's a whole story behind that.'

'I bet there is.' She glances around the room, to the door to the kitchen. 'So, this is the house you grew up in?'

'Yeah,' I say, looking around too. 'Lots of happy memories attached to this place.'

'How lovely. It's good to have plenty of those.' She has this way of saying things, even small things, as though she really means them.

'I'll just be a minute, then we can be on our way.' I run upstairs, go into Mum's bedroom and open the curtains that I closed last night. I go to the bathroom and switch the light on there. Mine and Pete's room next, where again I turn the light on, half close the curtains. There are no bunk beds here any more, it's just used for storing stuff, and Mum has her exercise bike in here. Even so, Mum still calls it *the boy's room*, and me and Pete, *our bedroom*. I'm sure we always will. 'Think I'm ready to go now,' I call.

'OK then,' she calls back.

Going downstairs, I see that Amber is already by the front door. I go to pick up my keys from the console table where I'd dropped them when we'd arrived, am about to walk down the hall when she holds her hands up to me.

'Stop right there,' she says.

I freeze. 'What's the matter?'

She glances above my head, then back down to me.

I look up, see the green leaves and white berries hanging from the ceiling. Mistletoe. There, in the same place Mum has hung a spray of this plant every Christmas that I can remember. And I laugh a little. I look to Amber, and I'm about to say something, but nothing comes out. I'm speechless, actually. I think she notices, as she smiles more, begins to come towards me. My heart is thumping. Perhaps there's nothing left to say right now.

Acknowledgements

A big thank you to Anne, Annemarie, Elise, Laura, Oana, Rob and Roger, for all your feedback and guidance in writing this story.

Thank you to Kathleen, Mandy and Michelle for your feedback on the early drafts, thanks to Richard for proofreading and to Ken for the wonderful cover.

Also by this author:

THE DECEIT BIRDS

THE GARDEN OF LONGING

for Ava and Jessica